MORE PRAISE FOR BABYMOUSE!

"Sassy, smart . . .
Babymouse is here
to stay."
—The Horn Book Magazine

"Young readers
will happily
fall in line."
—Kirkus Reviews

"The brother-sister creative team hits the mark
with humor, sweetness, and characters so genuine
they can pass for real kids." —Booklist

"Babymouse is spunky, ambitious,
and, at times, a total dweeb."
—School Library Journal

Be sure to read **all** the **BABYMOUSE** books:

#1 BABYMOUSE: Queen of the World!
#2 BABYMOUSE: Our Hero
#3 BABYMOUSE: Beach Babe
#4 BABYMOUSE: Rock Star
#5 BABYMOUSE: Heartbreaker
#6 CAMP BABYMOUSE
#7 BABYMOUSE: Skater Girl
#8 BABYMOUSE: Puppy Love
#9 BABYMOUSE: Monster Mash
#10 BABYMOUSE: The Musical
#11 BABYMOUSE: Dragonslayer

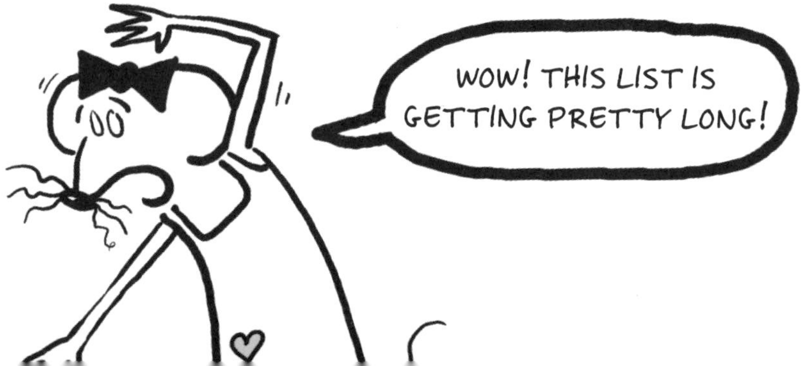
WOW! THIS LIST IS GETTING PRETTY LONG!

Dragonslayer

BY JENNIFER L. HOLM & MATTHEW HOLM

RANDOM HOUSE NEW YORK

HEY! I THINK THEY SHOULD PUT MATT'S NAME FIRST! HE DOES ALL THE DRAWING!

Published in the United States by Random House Children's Books, a division of Random House, Inc., New York.

Random House and the colophon are registered trademarks of Random House, Inc.

Visit us on the Web! www.randomhouse.com/kids
www.babymouse.com

Educators and librarians, for a variety of teaching tools, visit us at www.randomhouse.com/teachers

Library of Congress Cataloging-in-Publication Data
Holm, Jennifer L.
Babymouse : dragonslayer / by Jennifer L. Holm & Matthew Holm. — 1st ed.
  p. cm. — (Babymouse ; 11)
Summary: An imaginative mouse who likes to read heroic fantasy novels finds herself on the school math team as it prepares to compete for the coveted Golden Slide Rule.
ISBN 978-0-375-85712-6 (trade) — ISBN 978-0-375-95712-3 (lib. bdg.)
[1. Graphic novels. [1. Graphic novels. 2. Imagination—Fiction. 3. Mathematics—Fiction. 4. Contests—Fiction. 5. Schools—Fiction. 6. Mice—Fiction. 7. Animals—Fiction.]
I. Holm, Matthew. II. Title. III. Title: Dragonslayer.
PZ7.7.H65Baf 2009 741.5'973—dc22 2008051110

MANUFACTURED IN MALAYSIA   10 9 8 7 6 5 4 3   First Edition

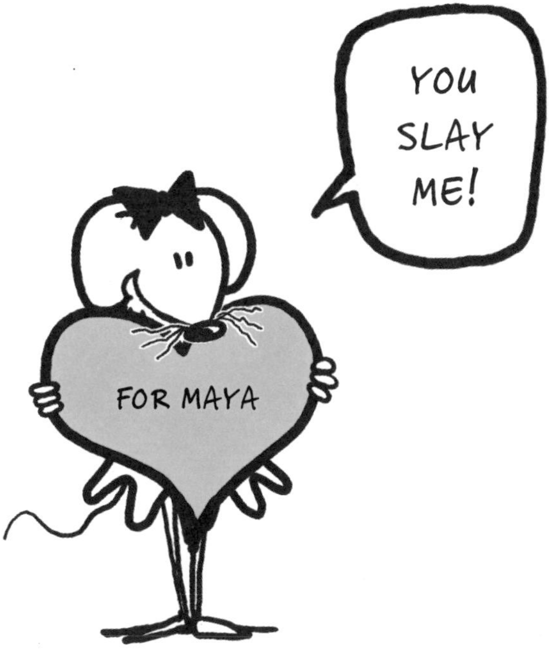
YOU SLAY ME!
FOR MAYA

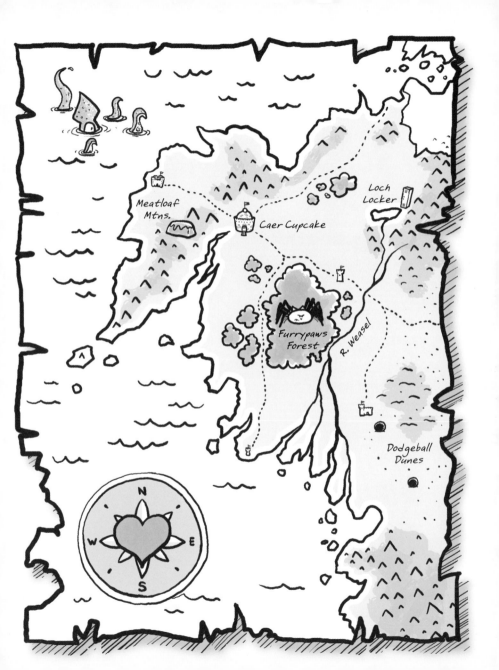

Meatloaf Mtns.

Caer Cupcake

Loch Locker

Furrypaws Forest

R. Weasel

Dodgeball Dunes

N
W   E
S

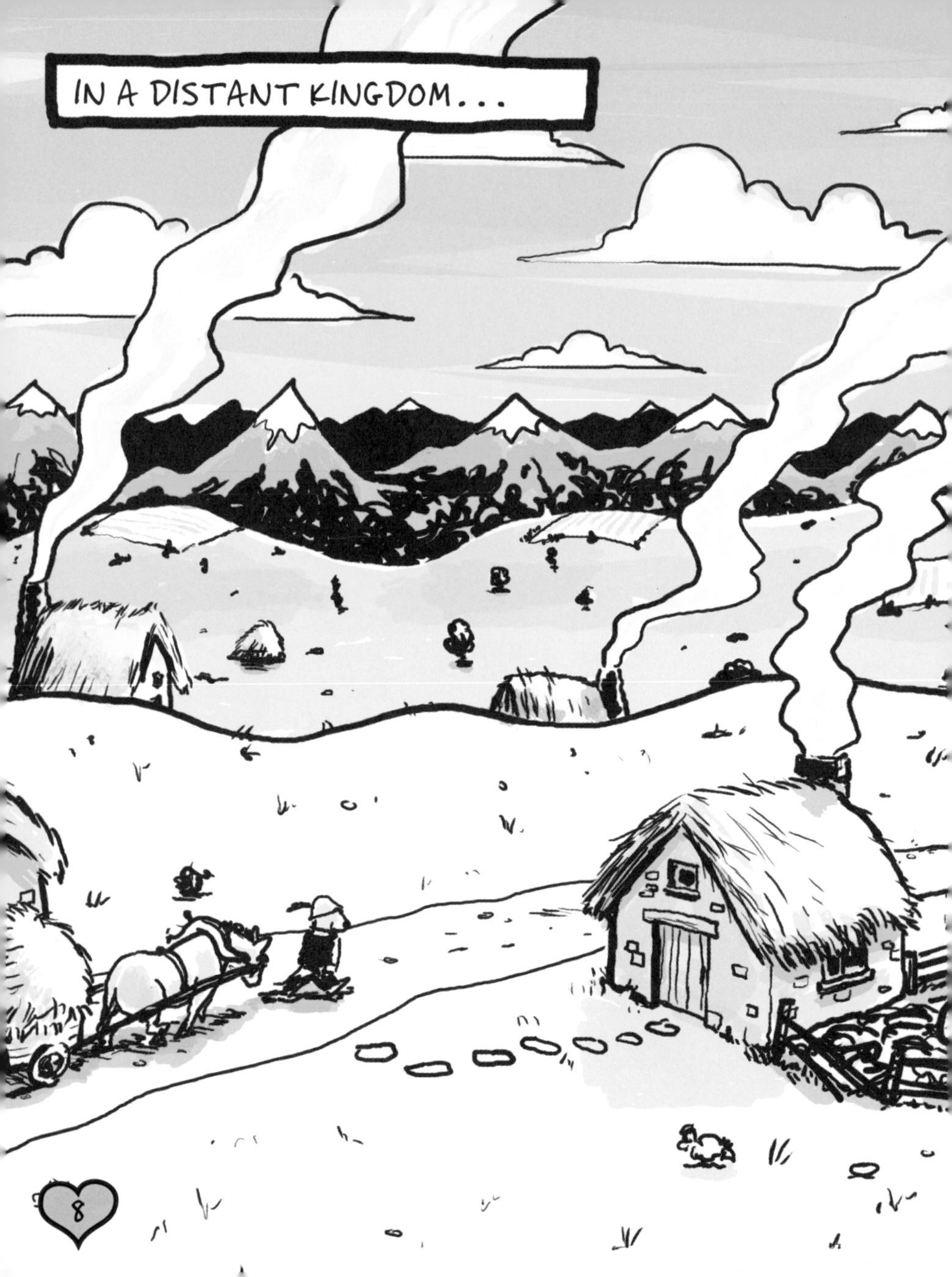
IN A DISTANT KINGDOM...

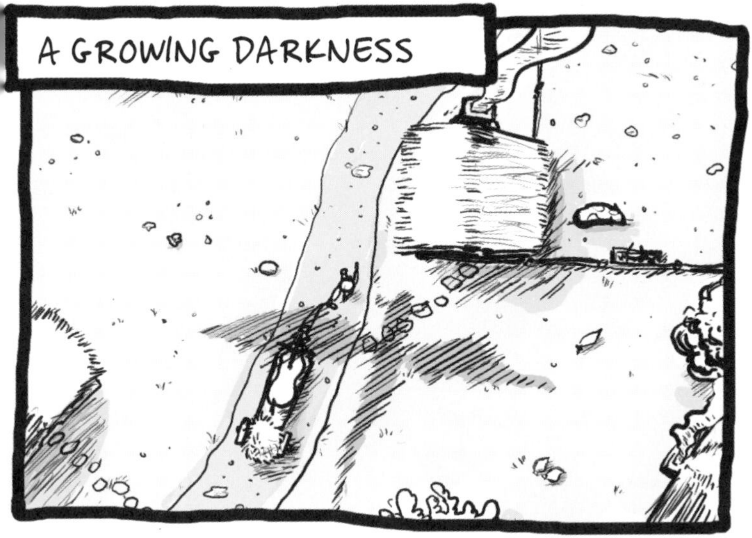
A GROWING DARKNESS

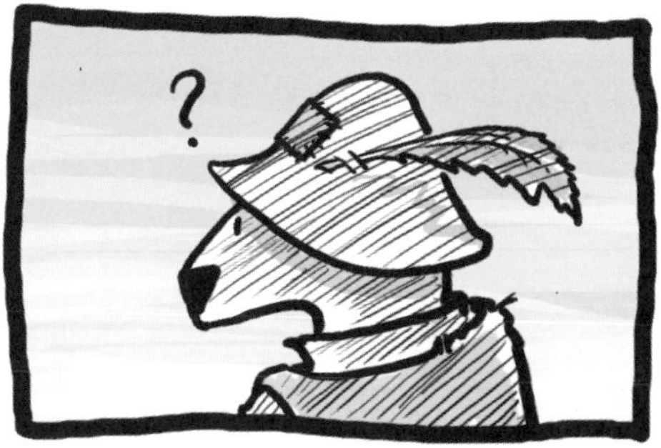
?

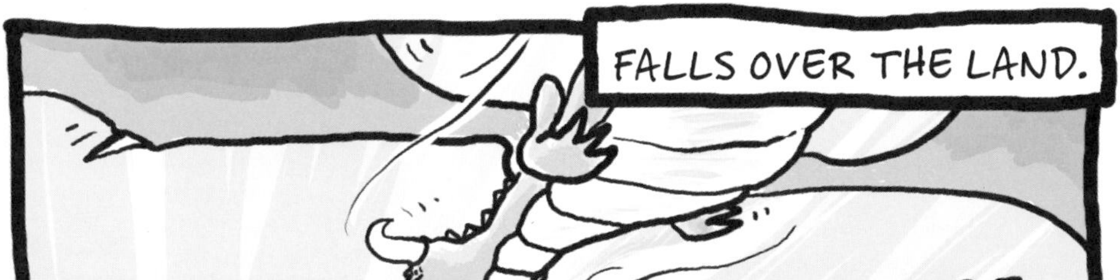
FALLS OVER THE LAND.
SWOOP!

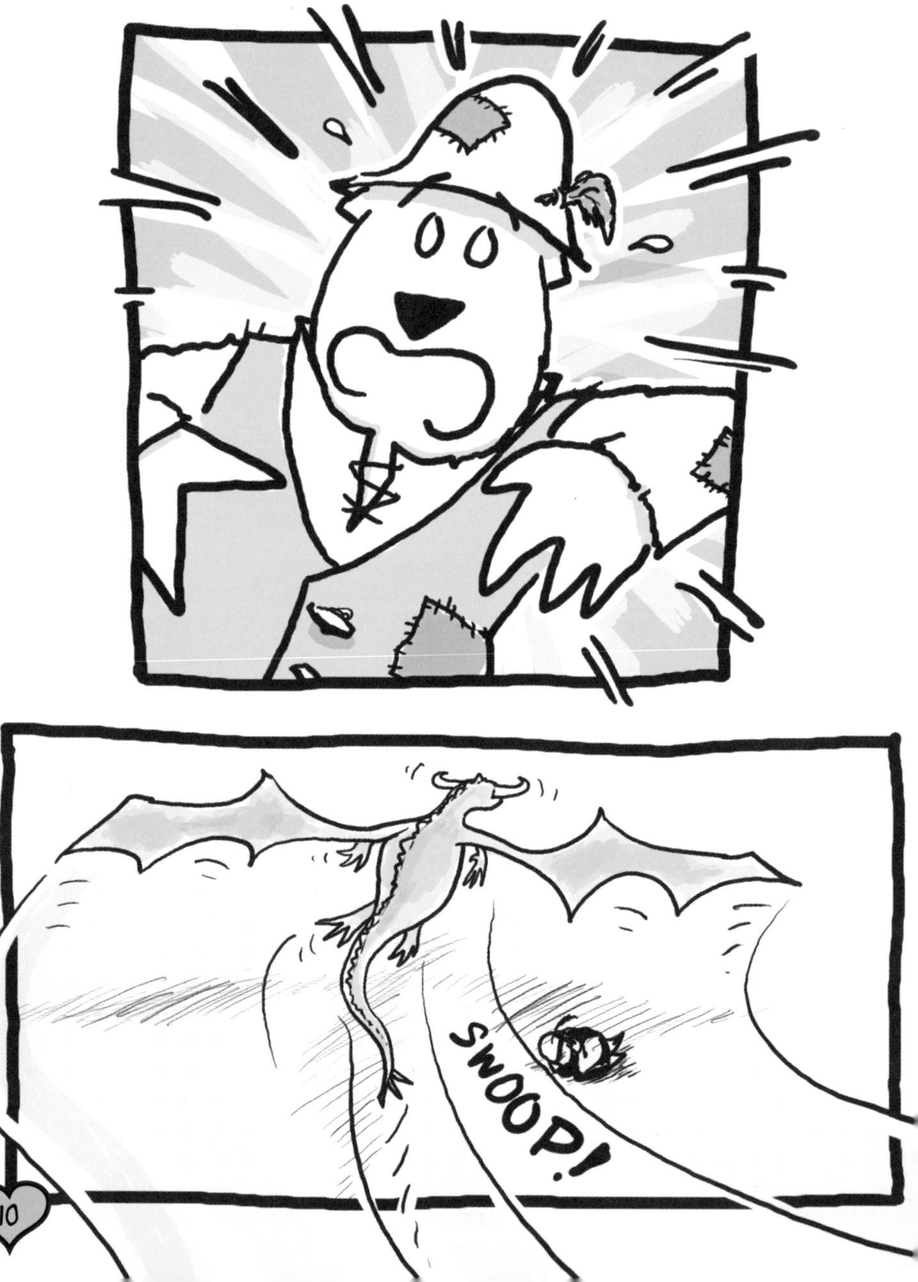
SWOOP!

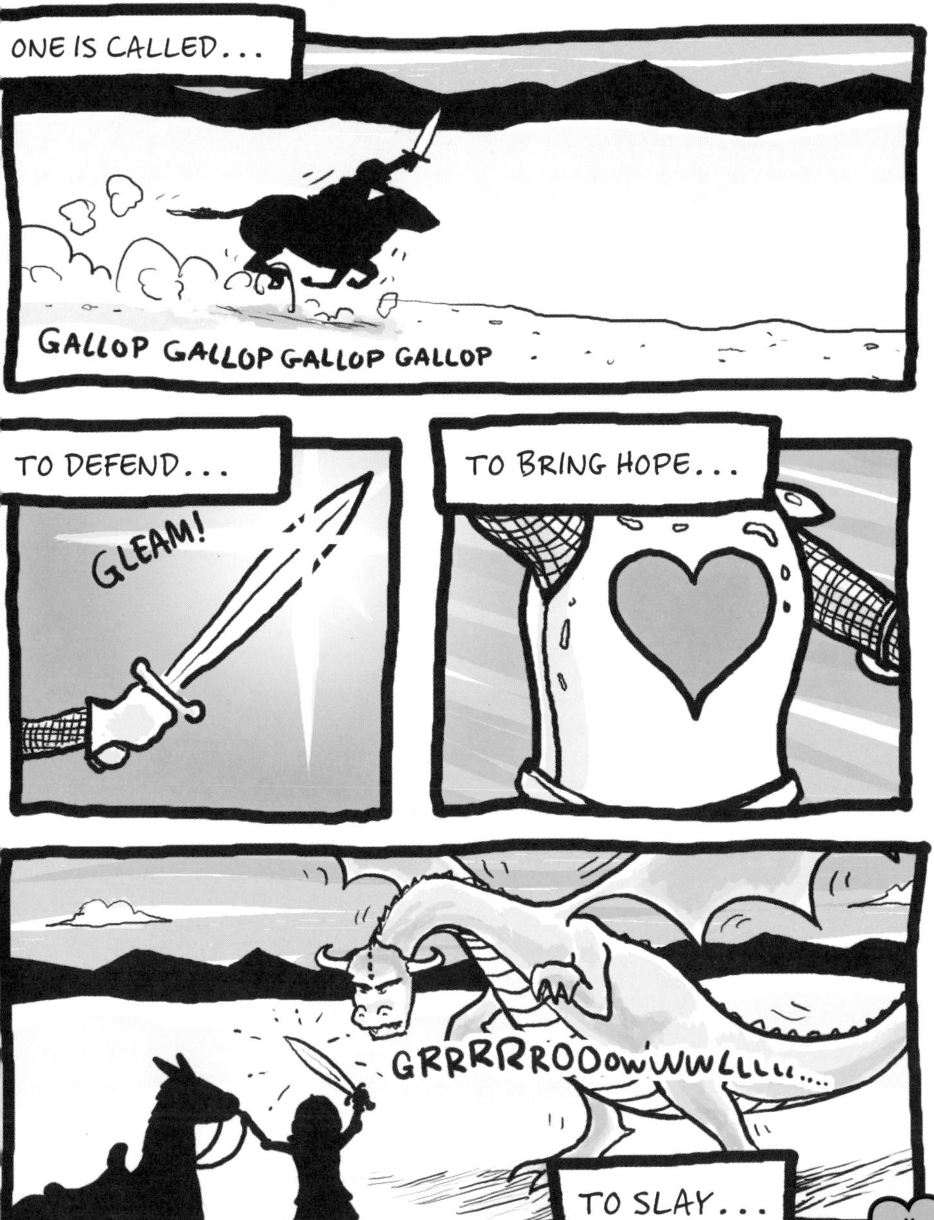
ONE IS CALLED...
GALLOP GALLOP GALLOP GALLOP
TO DEFEND...
GLEAM!
TO BRING HOPE...
GRRRRROOOOWWWLLLL....
TO SLAY...

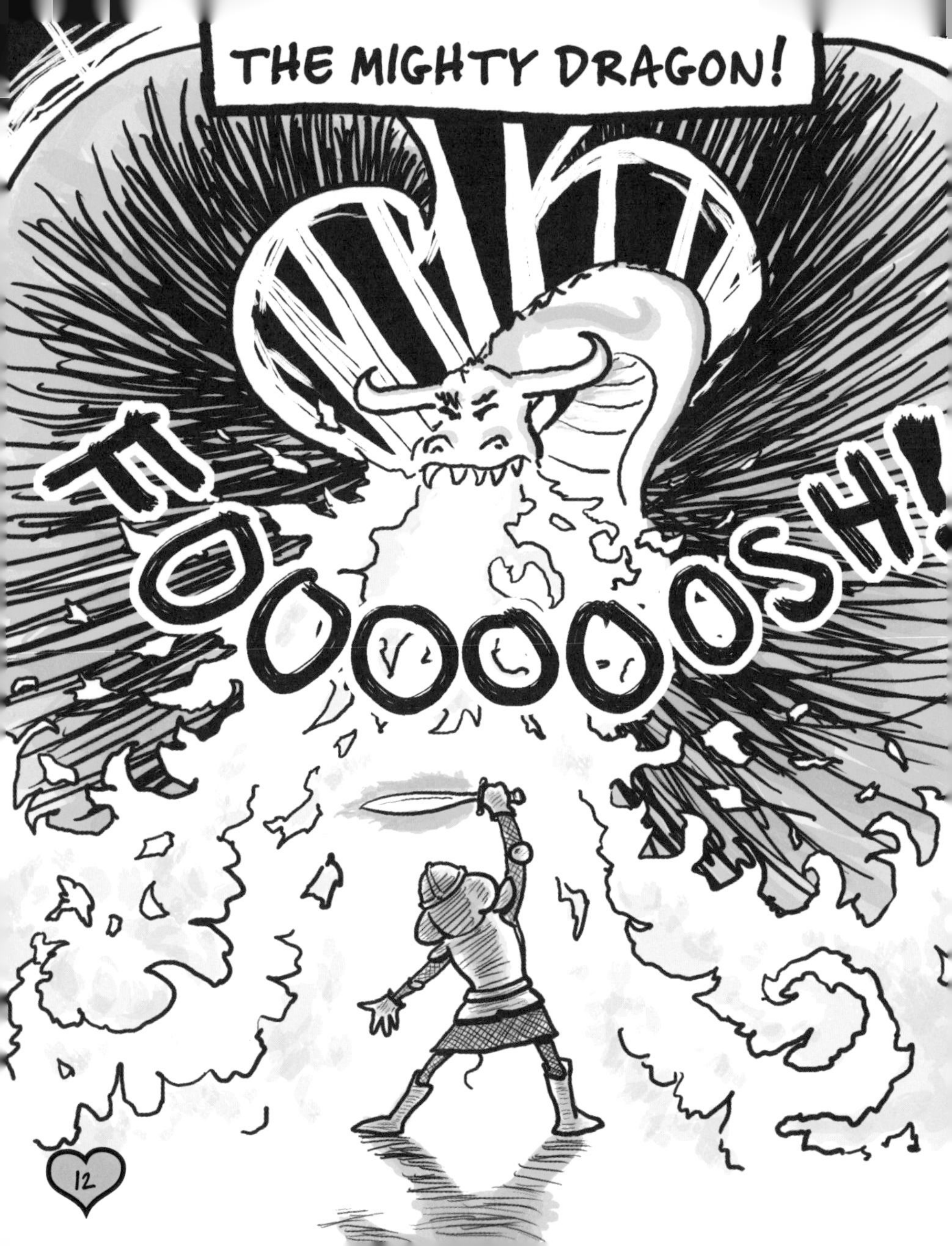
THE MIGHTY DRAGON!
FOOOOOOOSH!

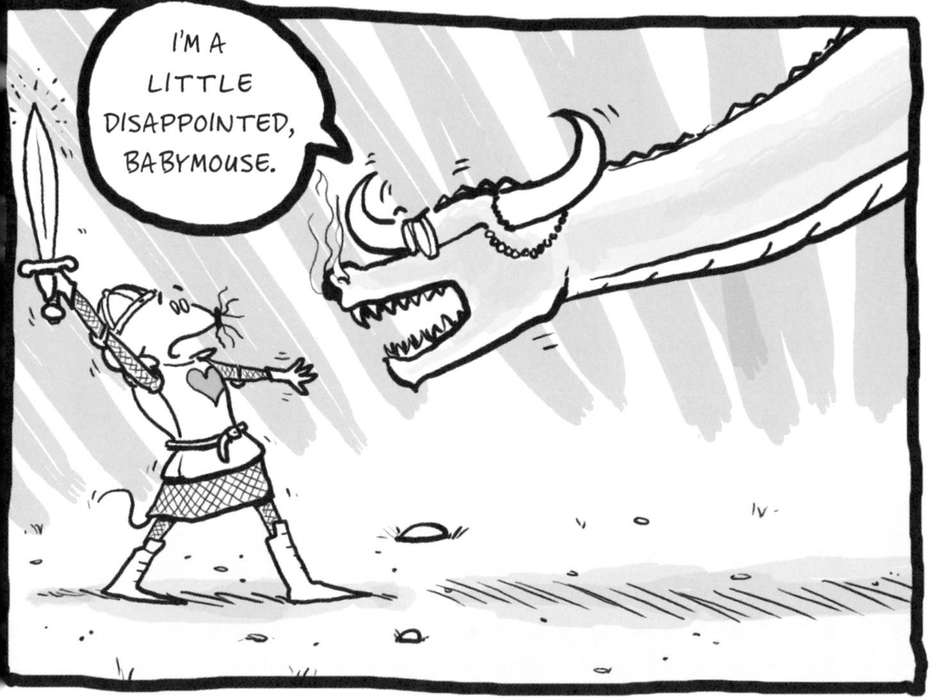
I'M A LITTLE DISAPPOINTED, BABYMOUSE.

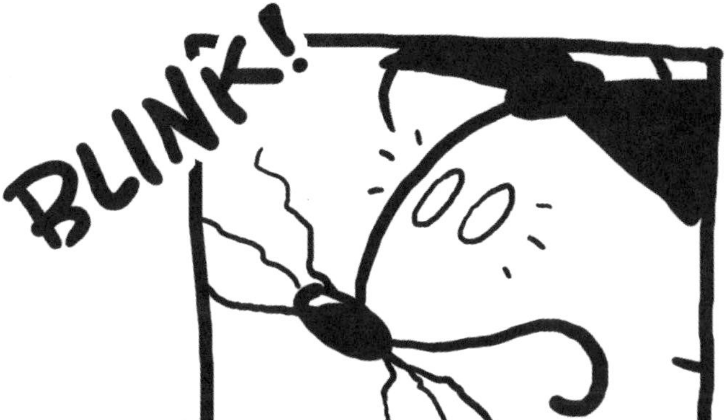
BLINK!

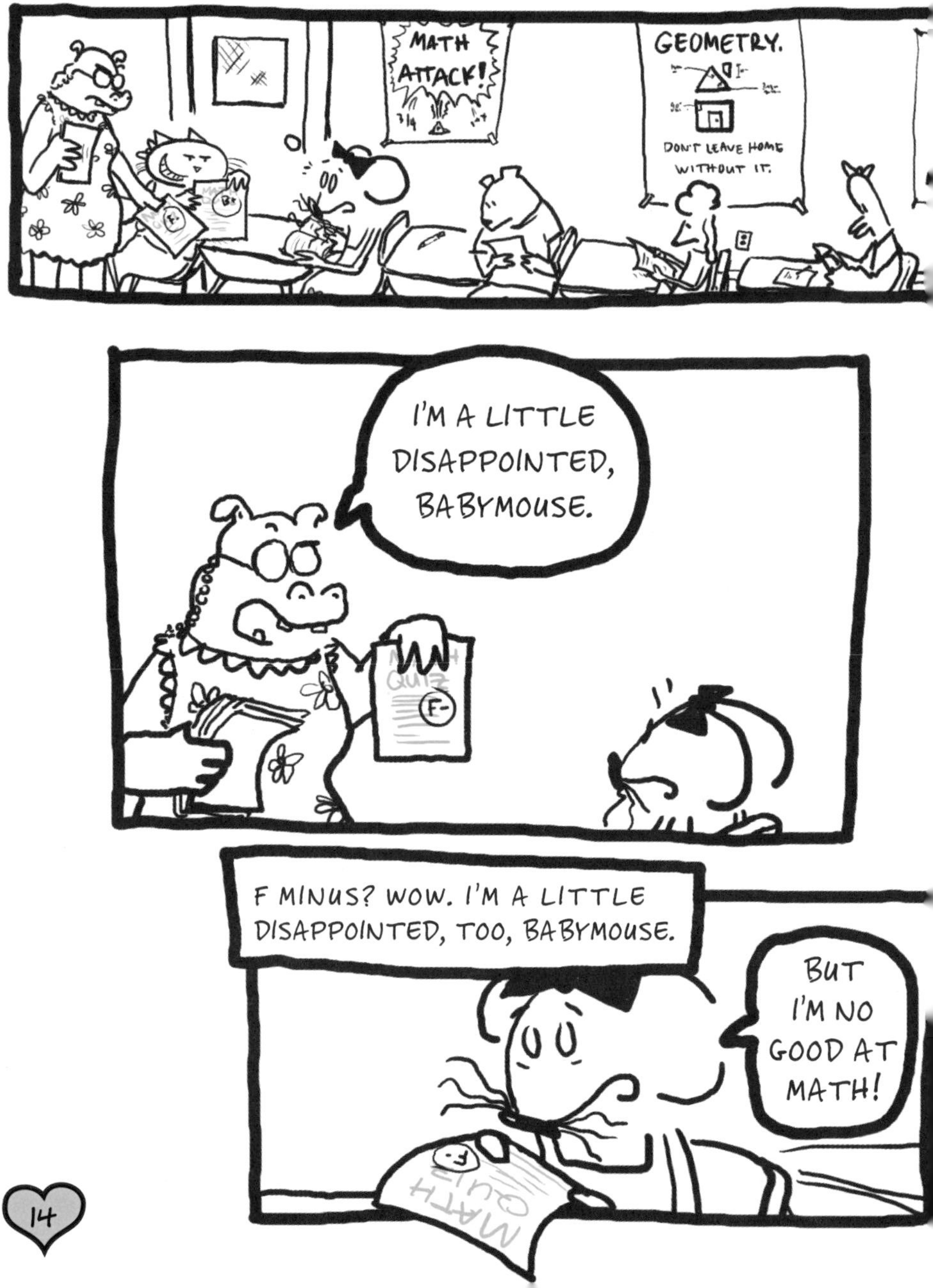
MATH ATTACK!
GEOMETRY.
DON'T LEAVE HOME WITHOUT IT.
I'M A LITTLE DISAPPOINTED, BABYMOUSE.
F MINUS? WOW. I'M A LITTLE DISAPPOINTED, TOO, BABYMOUSE.
BUT I'M NO GOOD AT MATH!

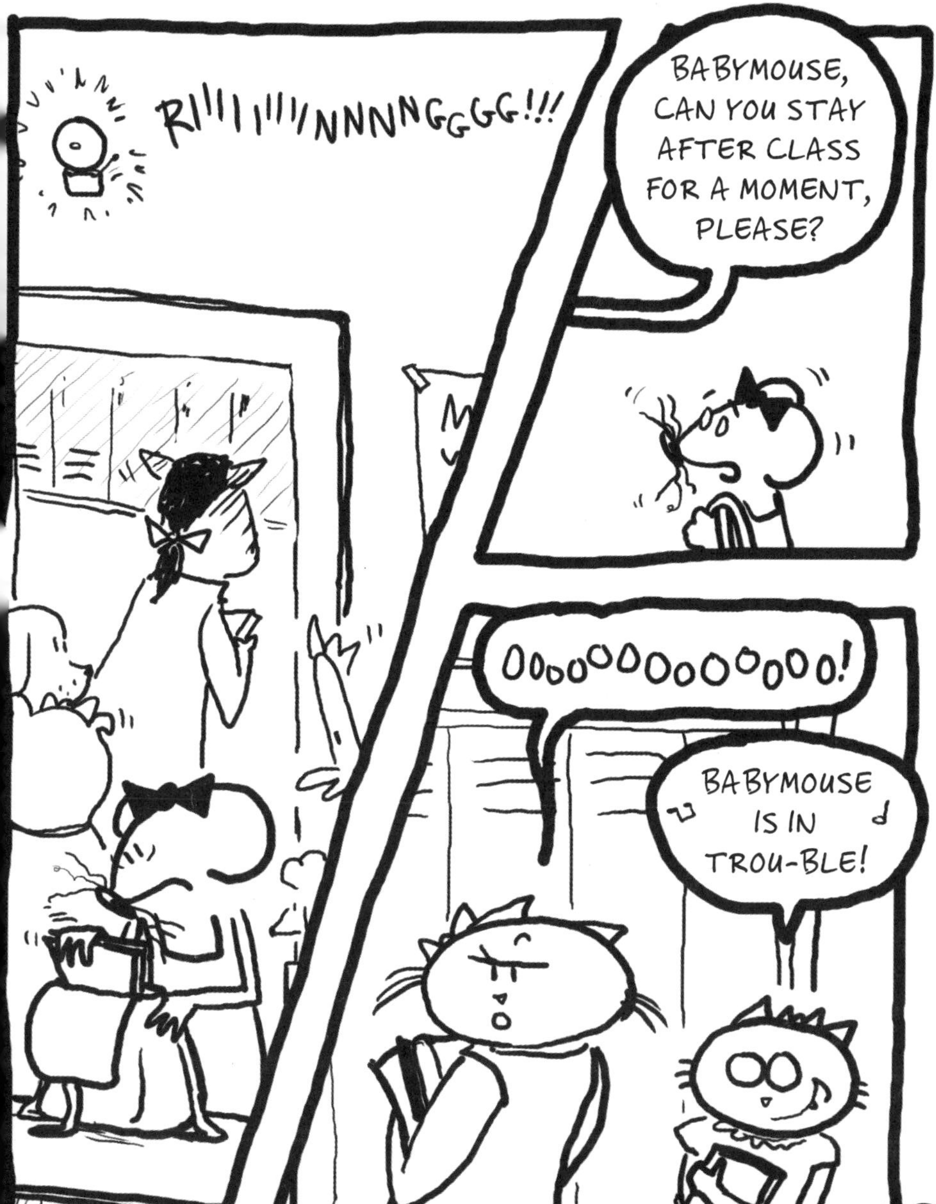
RIIIIIIIINNNNNGGGG!!!
BABYMOUSE, CAN YOU STAY AFTER CLASS FOR A MOMENT, PLEASE?
OOOOOOOOOOOOOO!
BABYMOUSE IS IN TROU-BLE!

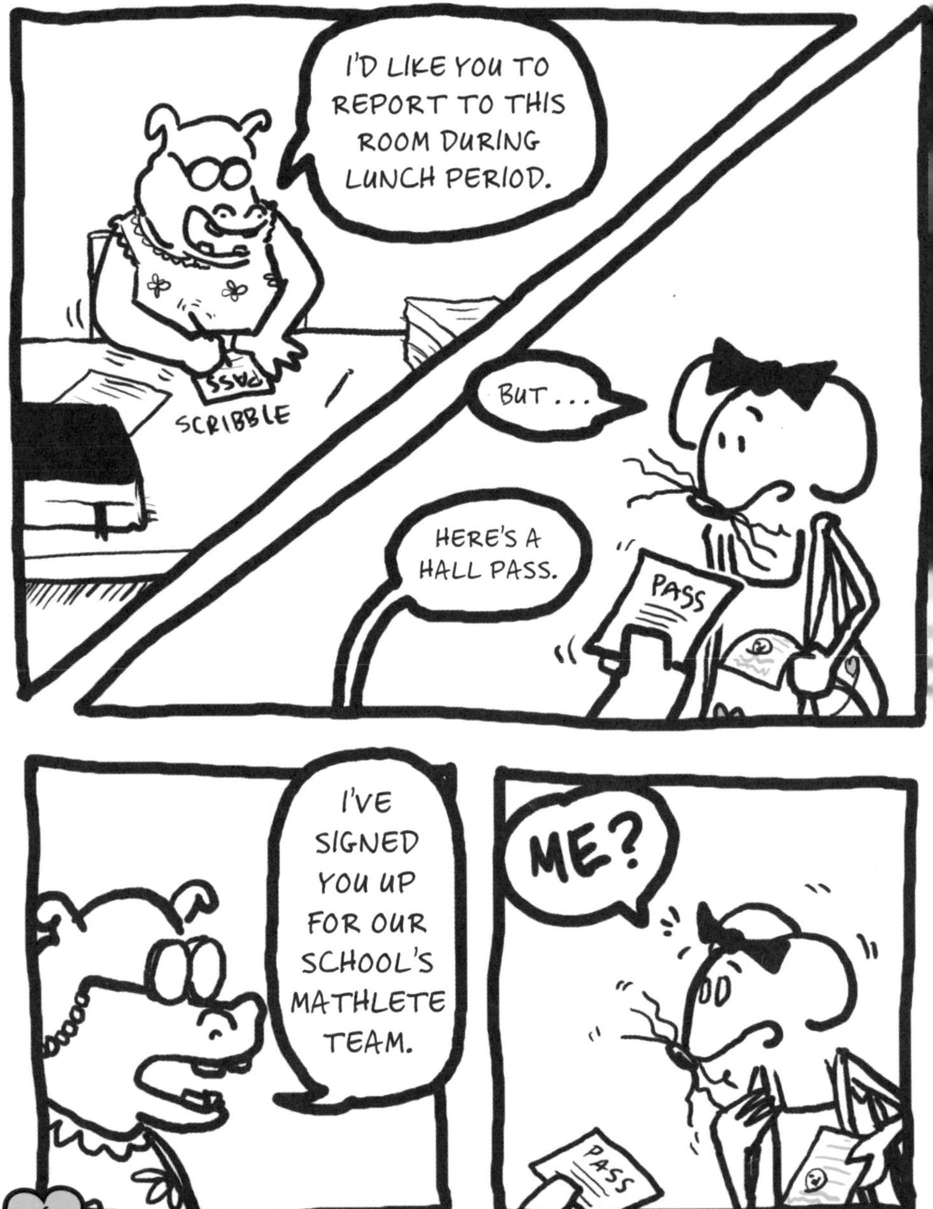
I'D LIKE YOU TO REPORT TO THIS ROOM DURING LUNCH PERIOD.
PASS
SCRIBBLE
BUT . . .
HERE'S A HALL PASS.
PASS
I'VE SIGNED YOU UP FOR OUR SCHOOL'S MATHLETE TEAM.
ME?
PASS

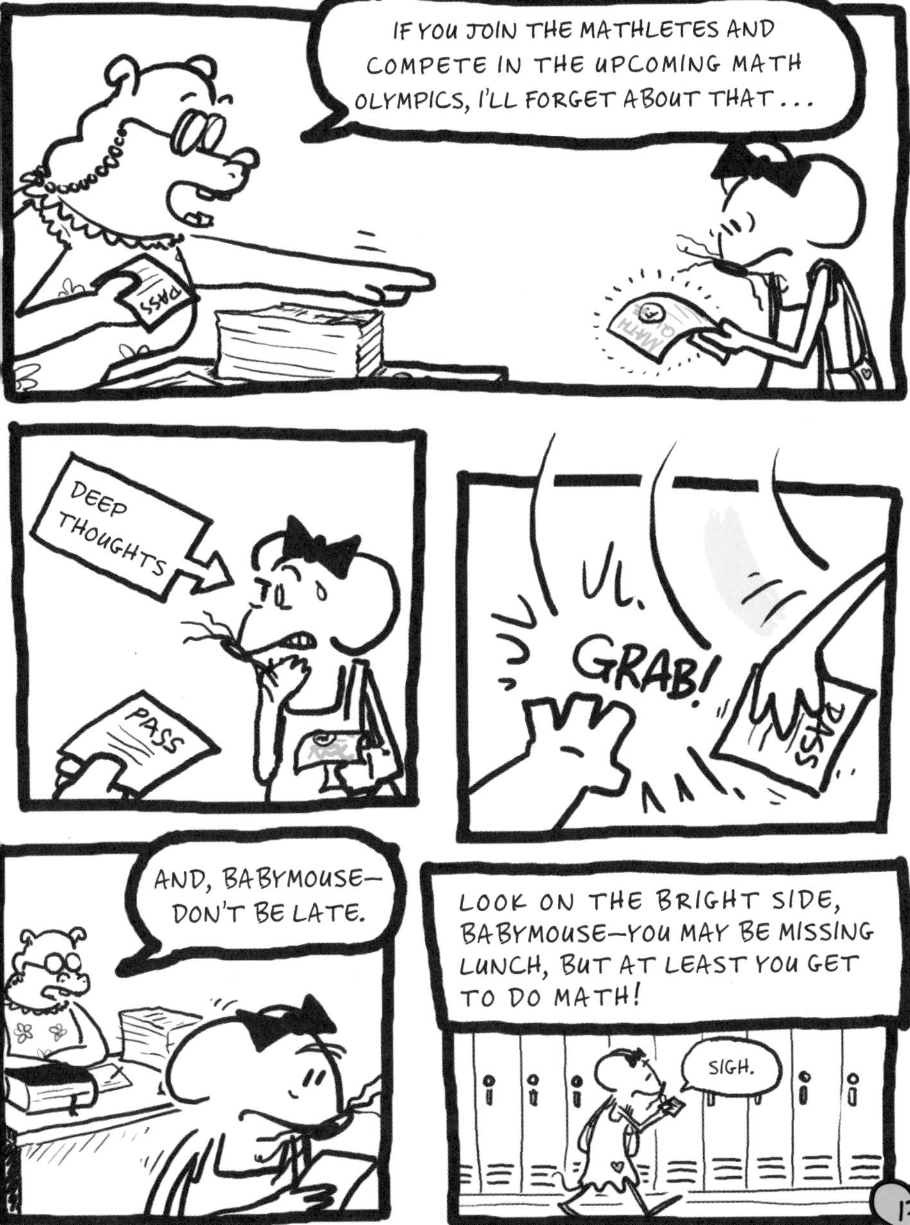
IF YOU JOIN THE MATHLETES AND COMPETE IN THE UPCOMING MATH OLYMPICS, I'LL FORGET ABOUT THAT . . .
PASS
MATH QUIZ
DEEP THOUGHTS
PASS
GRAB!
PASS
AND, BABYMOUSE—DON'T BE LATE.
LOOK ON THE BRIGHT SIDE, BABYMOUSE—YOU MAY BE MISSING LUNCH, BUT AT LEAST YOU GET TO DO MATH!
SIGH.

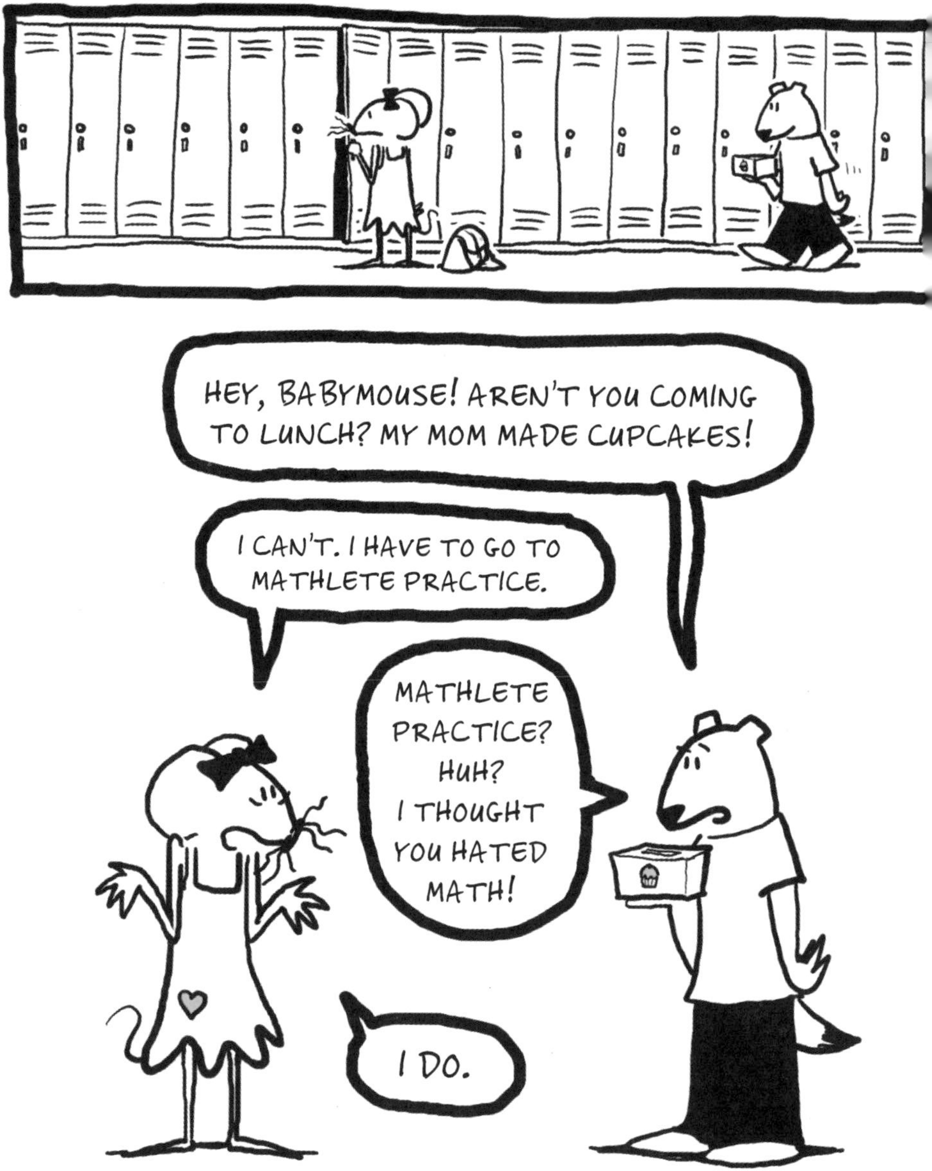
HEY, BABYMOUSE! AREN'T YOU COMING TO LUNCH? MY MOM MADE CUPCAKES!
I CAN'T. I HAVE TO GO TO MATHLETE PRACTICE.
MATHLETE PRACTICE? HUH? I THOUGHT YOU HATED MATH!
I DO.

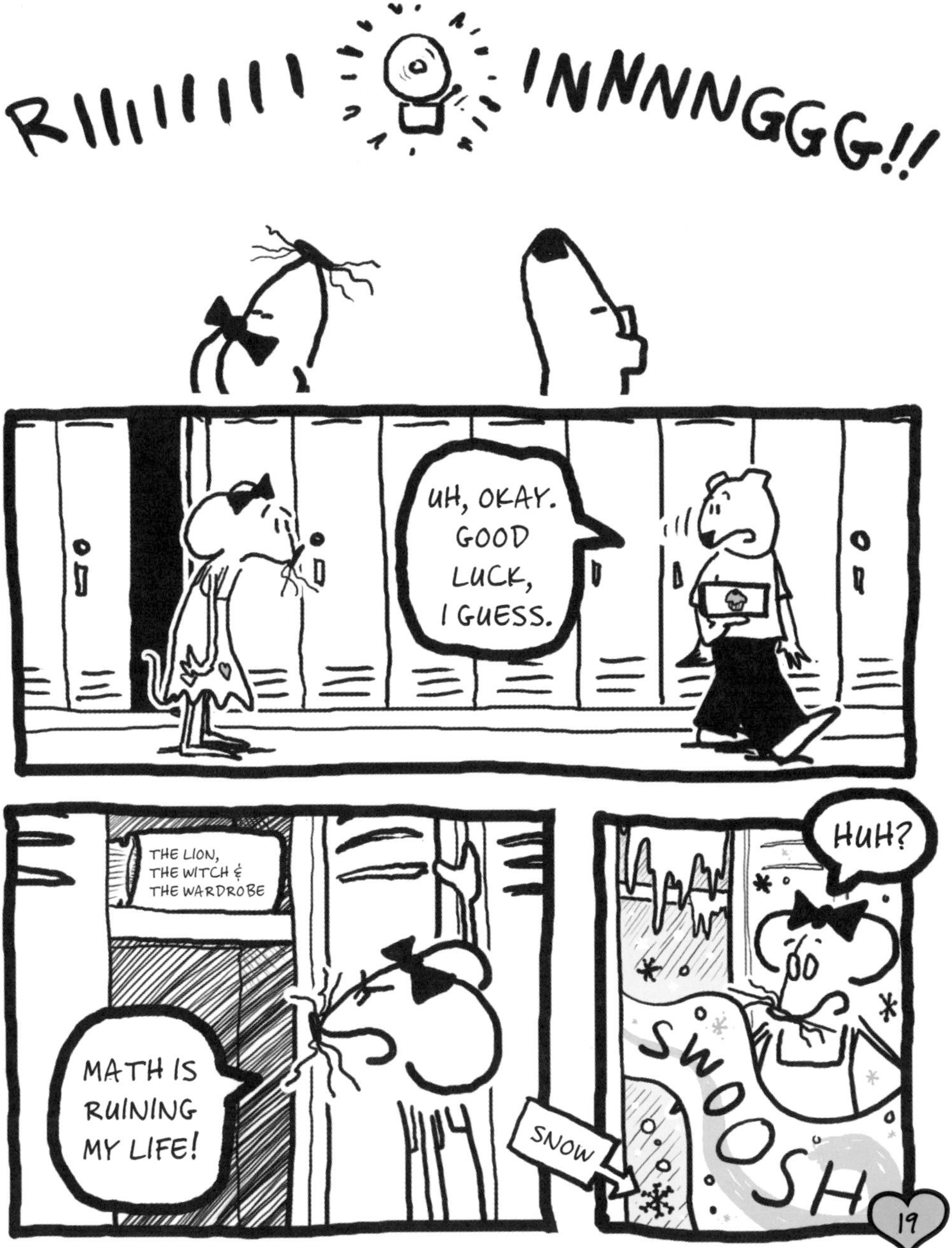

RIIIIIIII INNNNGGG!!
UH, OKAY. GOOD LUCK, I GUESS.
THE LION, THE WITCH & THE WARDROBE
MATH IS RUINING MY LIFE!
HUH?
SWOOSH
SNOW

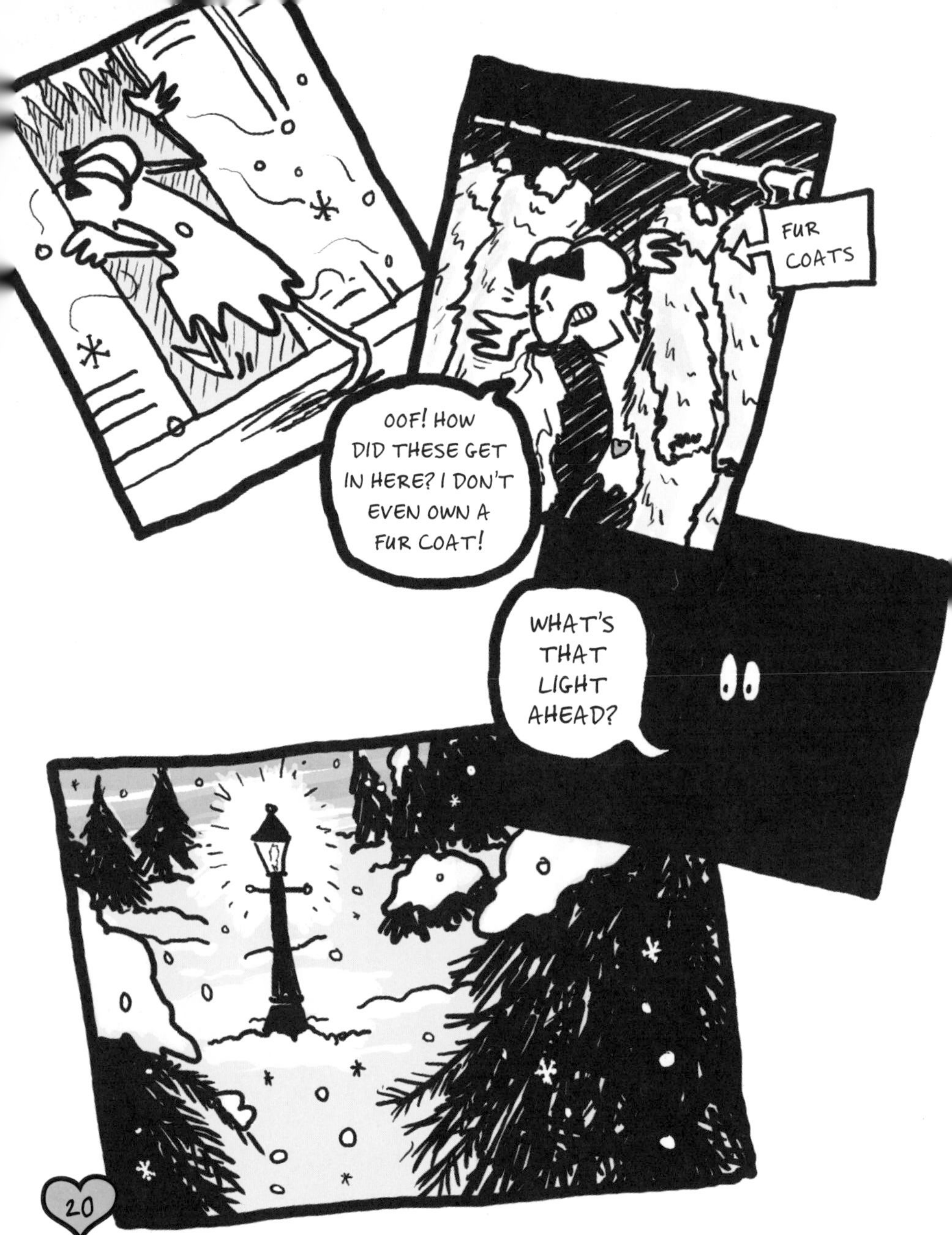
FUR COATS
OOF! HOW DID THESE GET IN HERE? I DON'T EVEN OWN A FUR COAT!
WHAT'S THAT LIGHT AHEAD?

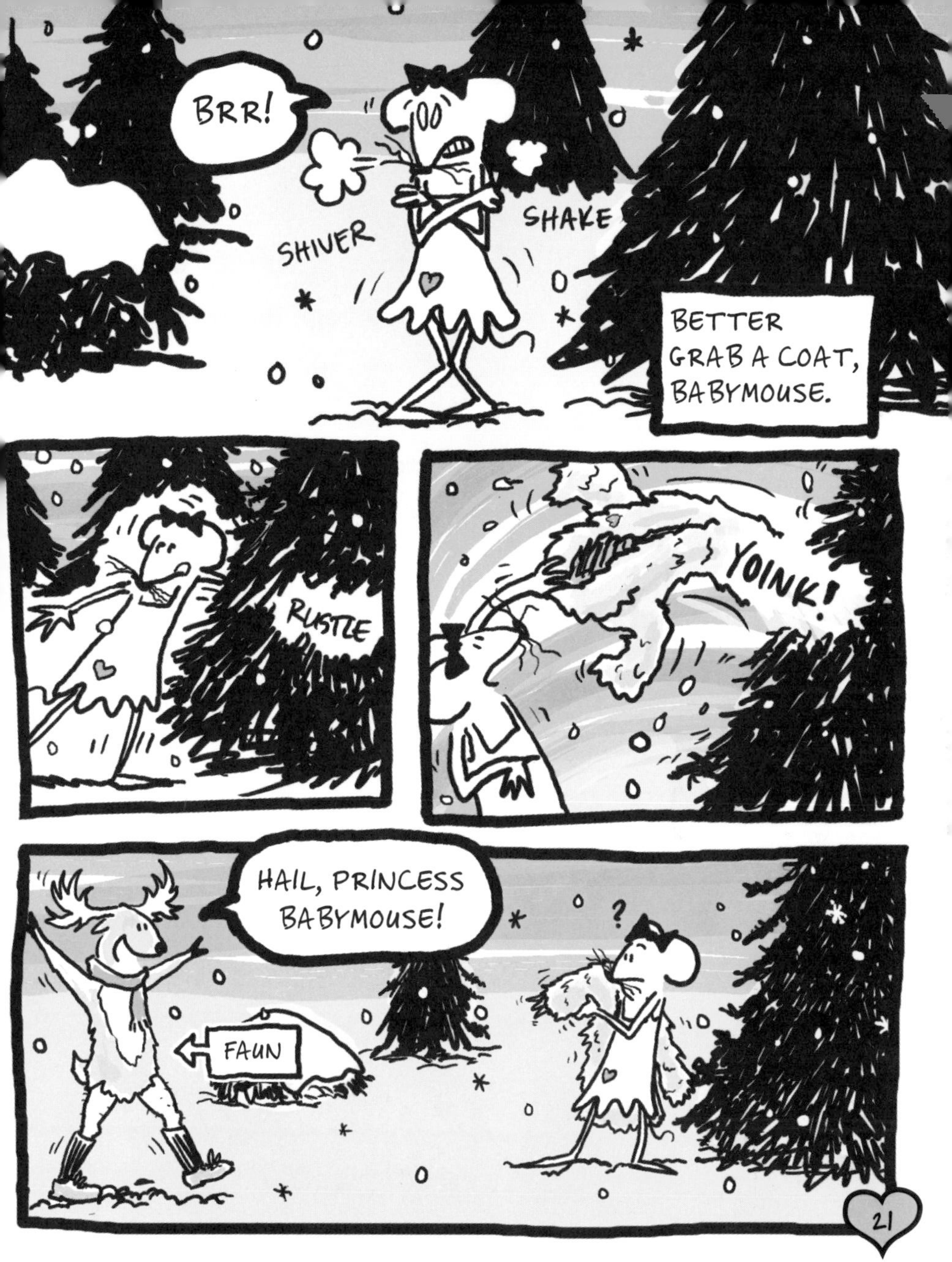
BRR!
SHIVER
SHAKE
BETTER GRAB A COAT, BABYMOUSE.
RUSTLE
YOINK!
HAIL, PRINCESS BABYMOUSE!
?
FAUN

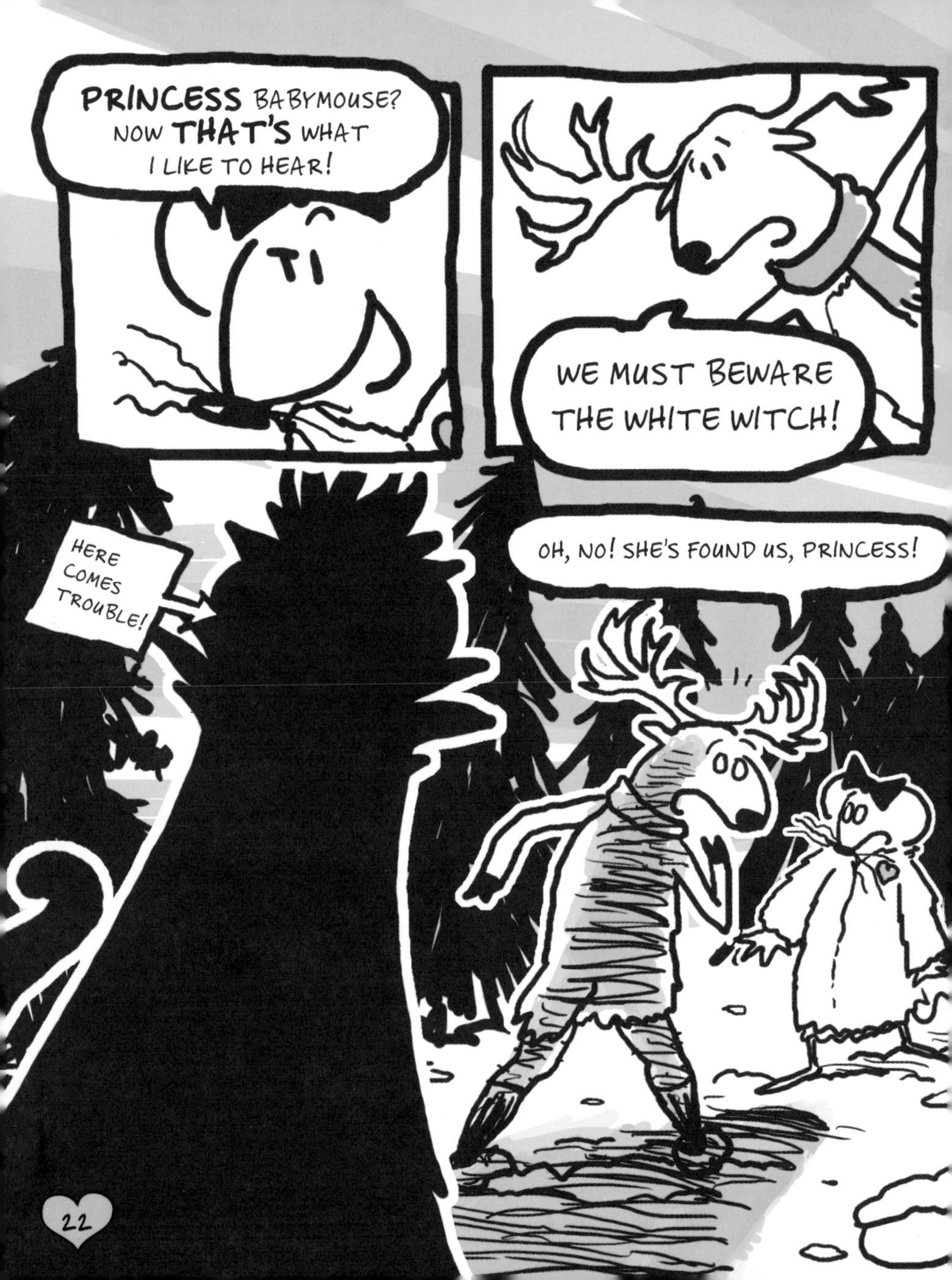

PRINCESS BABYMOUSE? NOW THAT'S WHAT I LIKE TO HEAR!
WE MUST BEWARE THE WHITE WITCH!
HERE COMES TROUBLE!
OH, NO! SHE'S FOUND US, PRINCESS!

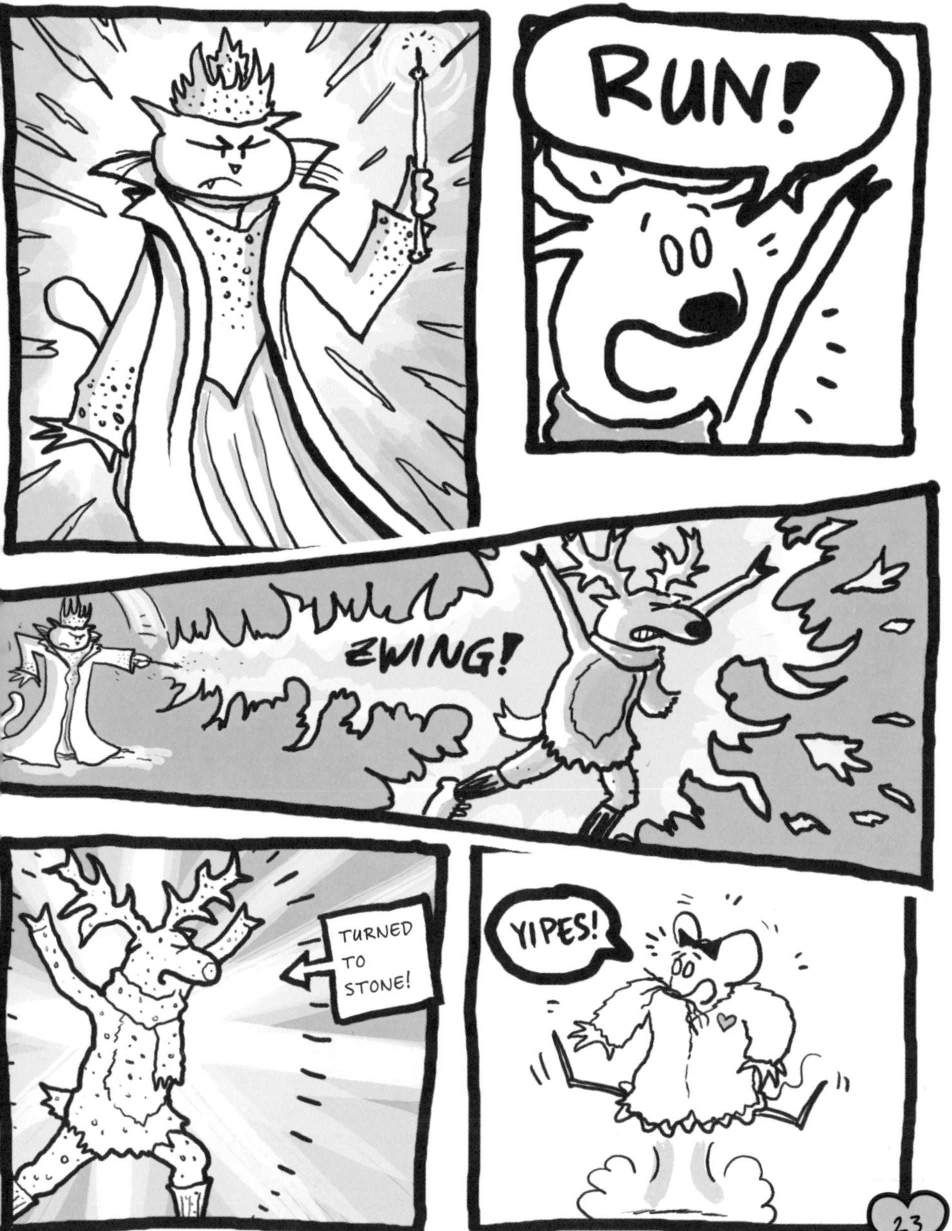
RUN!
ZWING!
TURNED TO STONE!
YIPES!

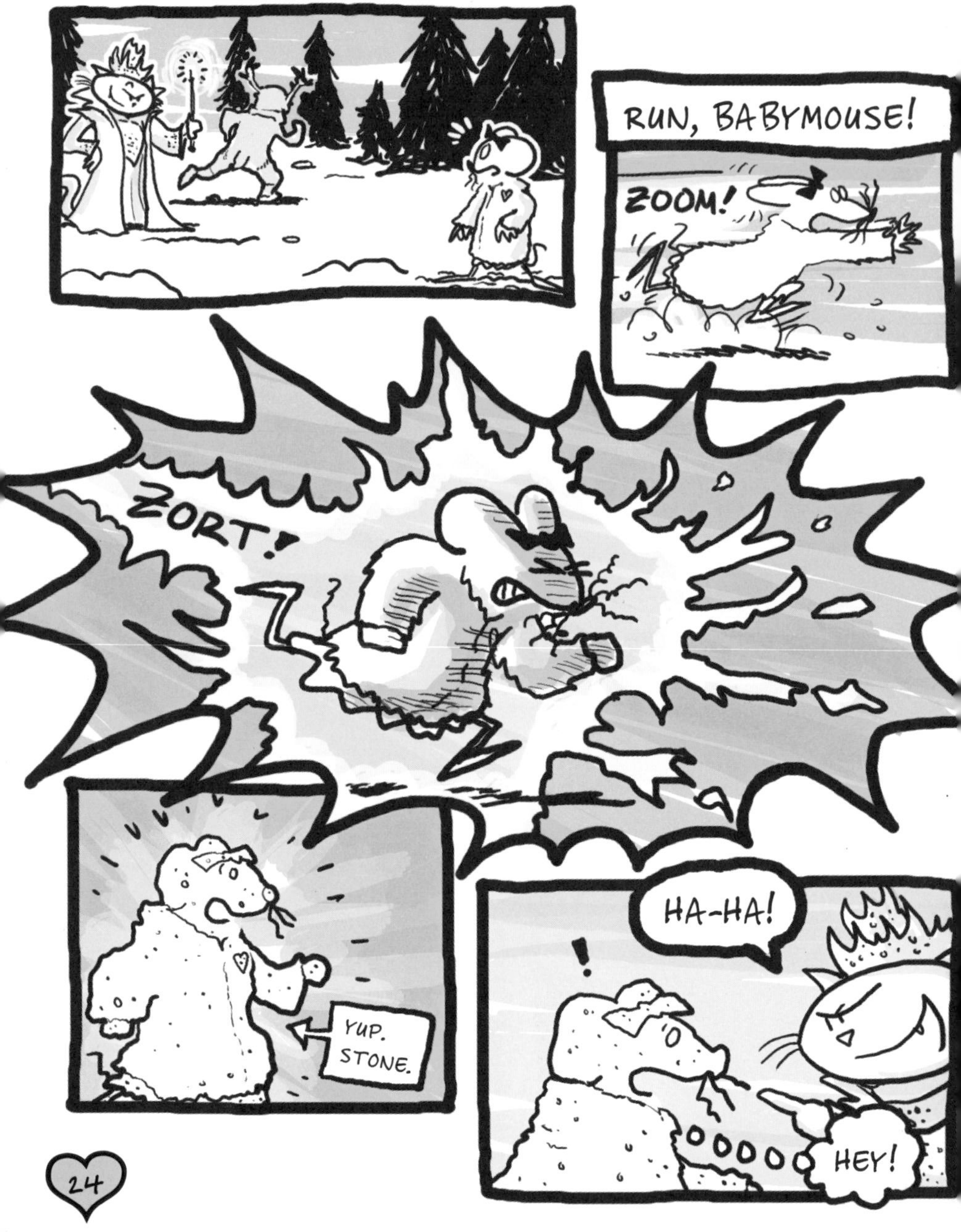
RUN, BABYMOUSE!
ZOOM!
ZORT!
YUP. STONE.
HA-HA!
!
OOOOO
HEY!

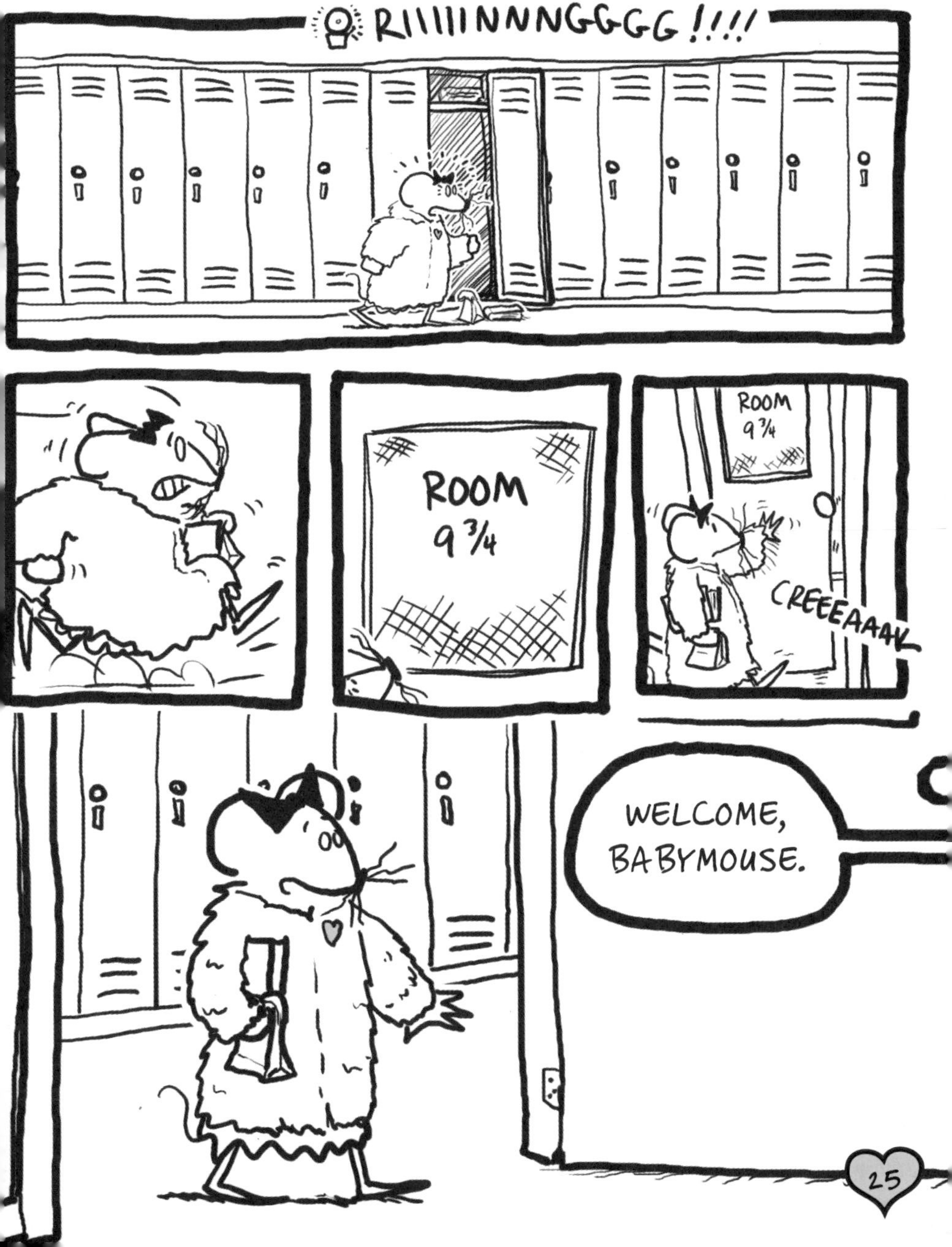
RIIIIINNNGGGG!!!!
ROOM 9 3/4
ROOM 9 3/4
CREEEEAAAK
WELCOME, BABYMOUSE.

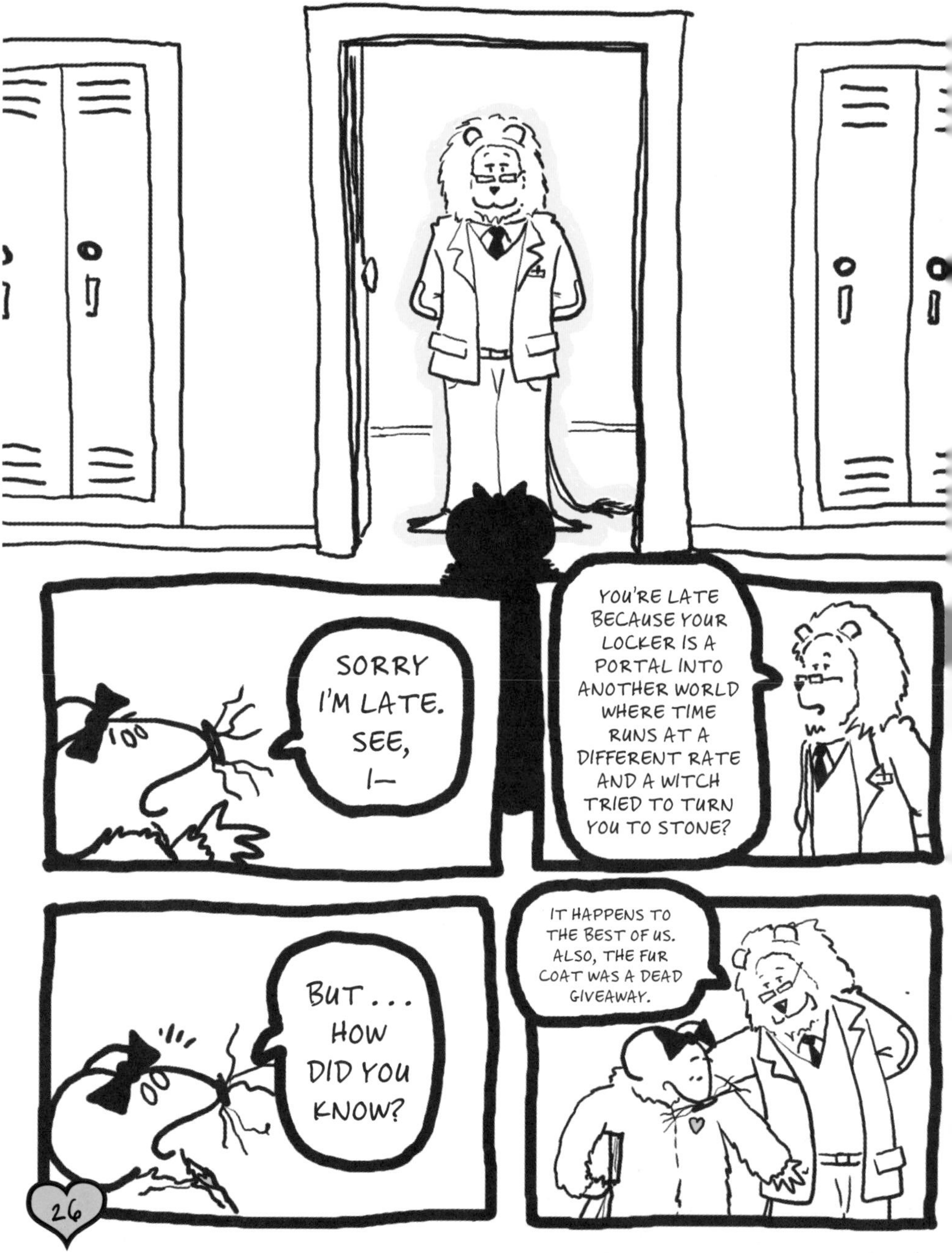
SORRY I'M LATE. SEE, I—
YOU'RE LATE BECAUSE YOUR LOCKER IS A PORTAL INTO ANOTHER WORLD WHERE TIME RUNS AT A DIFFERENT RATE AND A WITCH TRIED TO TURN YOU TO STONE?
BUT . . . HOW DID YOU KNOW?
IT HAPPENS TO THE BEST OF US. ALSO, THE FUR COAT WAS A DEAD GIVEAWAY.

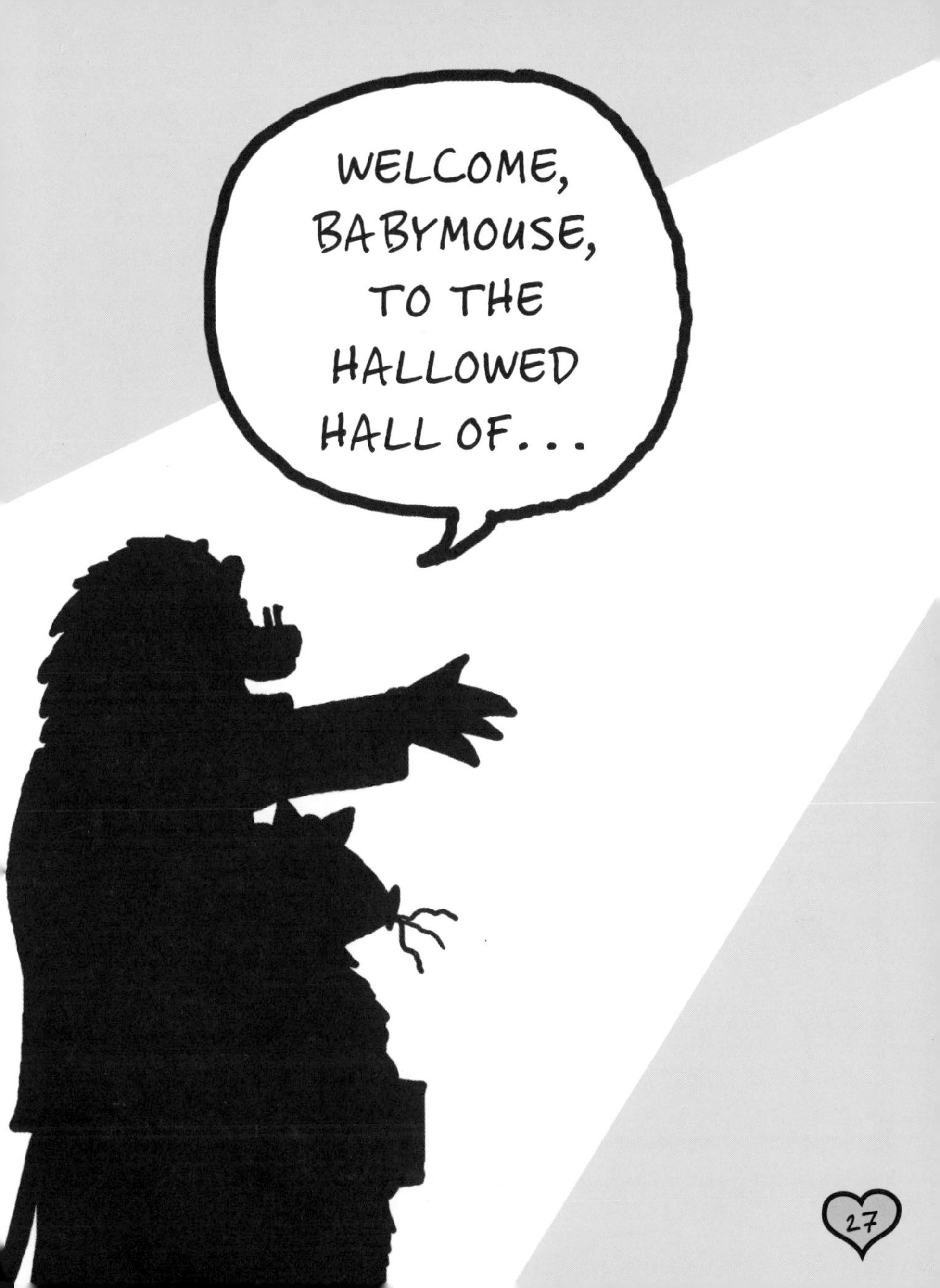
WELCOME, BABYMOUSE, TO THE HALLOWED HALL OF...

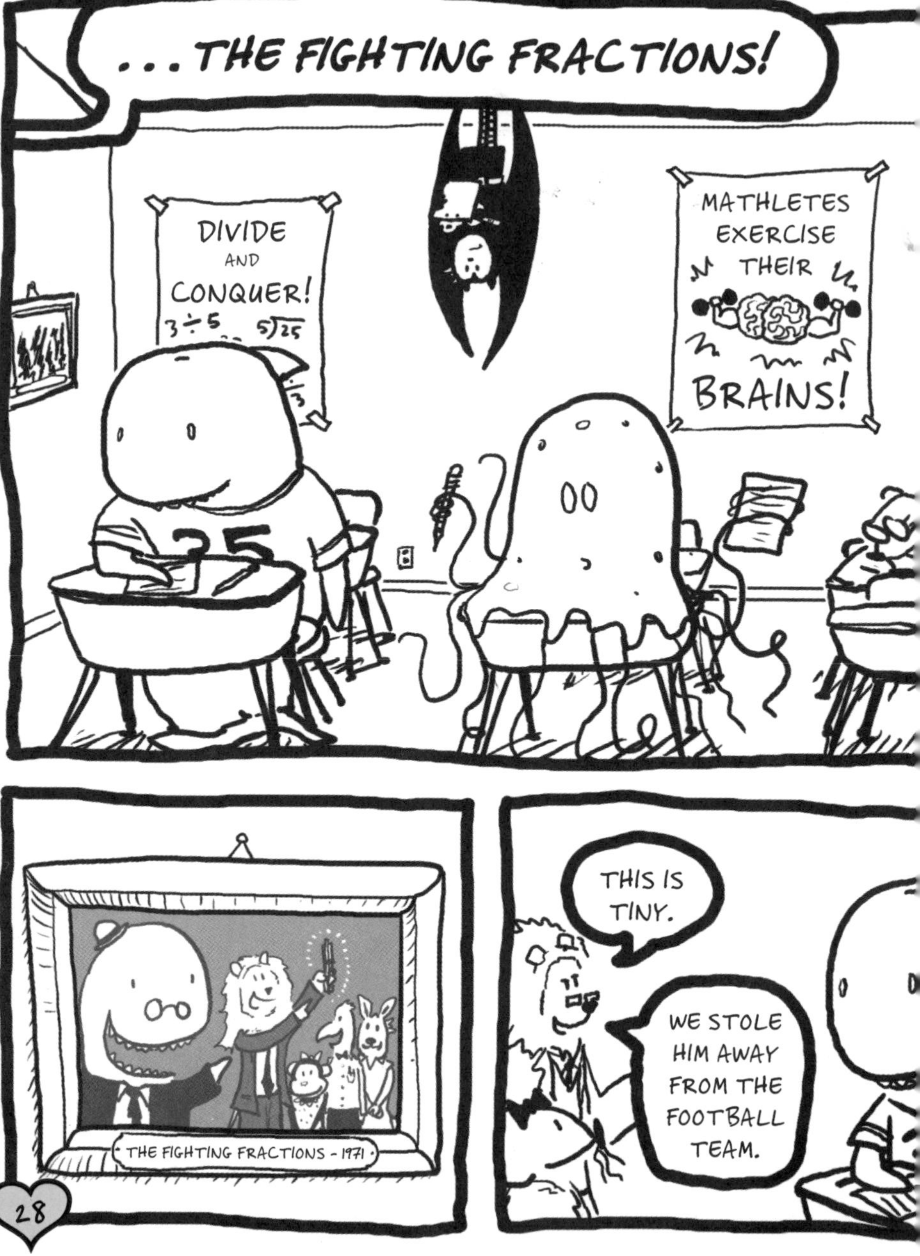
...THE FIGHTING FRACTIONS!
DIVIDE AND CONQUER!
MATHLETES EXERCISE THEIR BRAINS!
THE FIGHTING FRACTIONS - 1971
THIS IS TINY.
WE STOLE HIM AWAY FROM THE FOOTBALL TEAM.

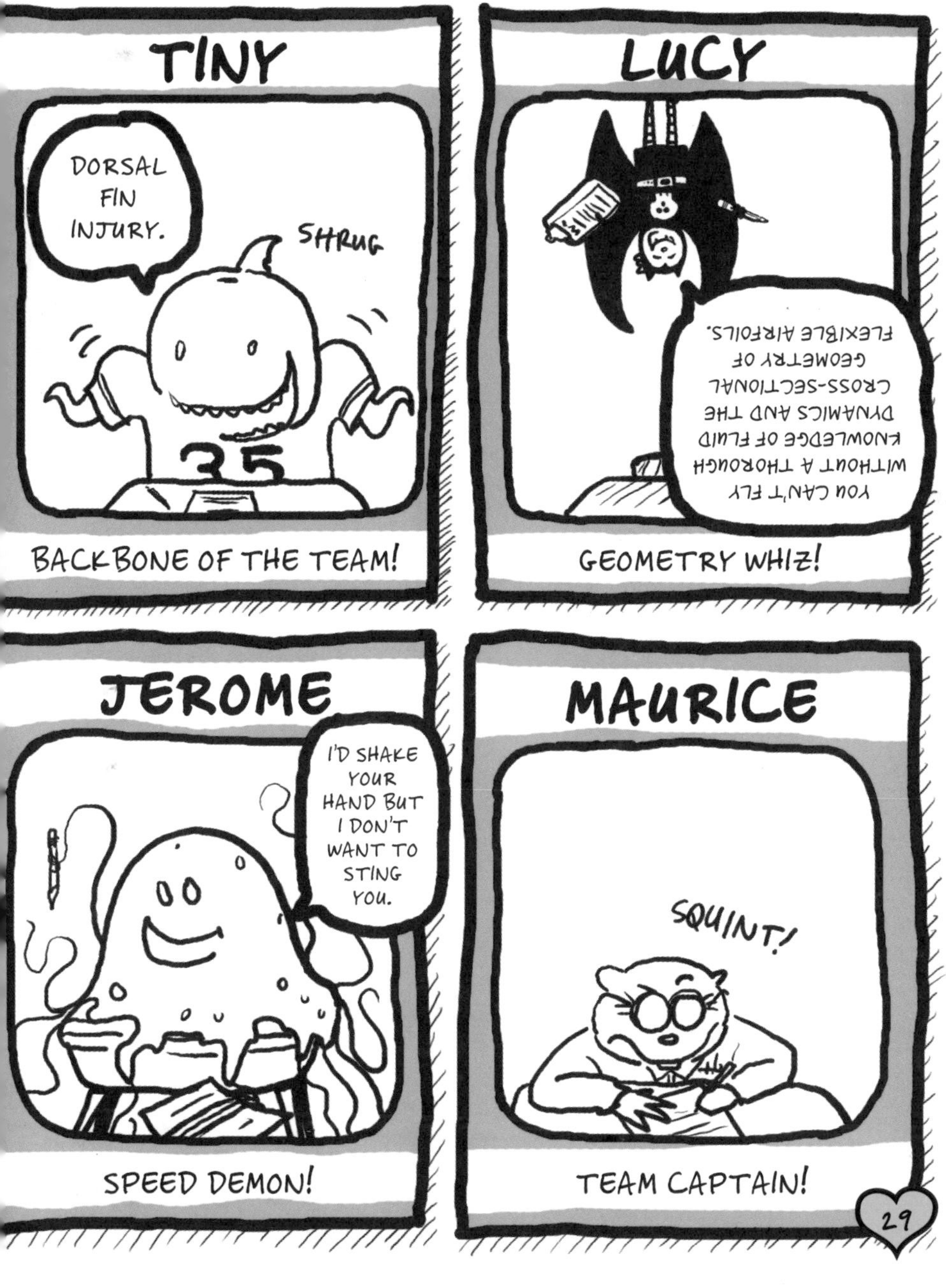
TINY
DORSAL FIN INJURY.
SHRUG
35
BACKBONE OF THE TEAM!
LUCY
YOU CAN'T FLY WITHOUT A THOROUGH KNOWLEDGE OF FLUID DYNAMICS AND THE CROSS-SECTIONAL GEOMETRY OF FLEXIBLE AIRFOILS.
GEOMETRY WHIZ!
JEROME
I'D SHAKE YOUR HAND BUT I DON'T WANT TO STING YOU.
SPEED DEMON!
MAURICE
SQUINT!
TEAM CAPTAIN!

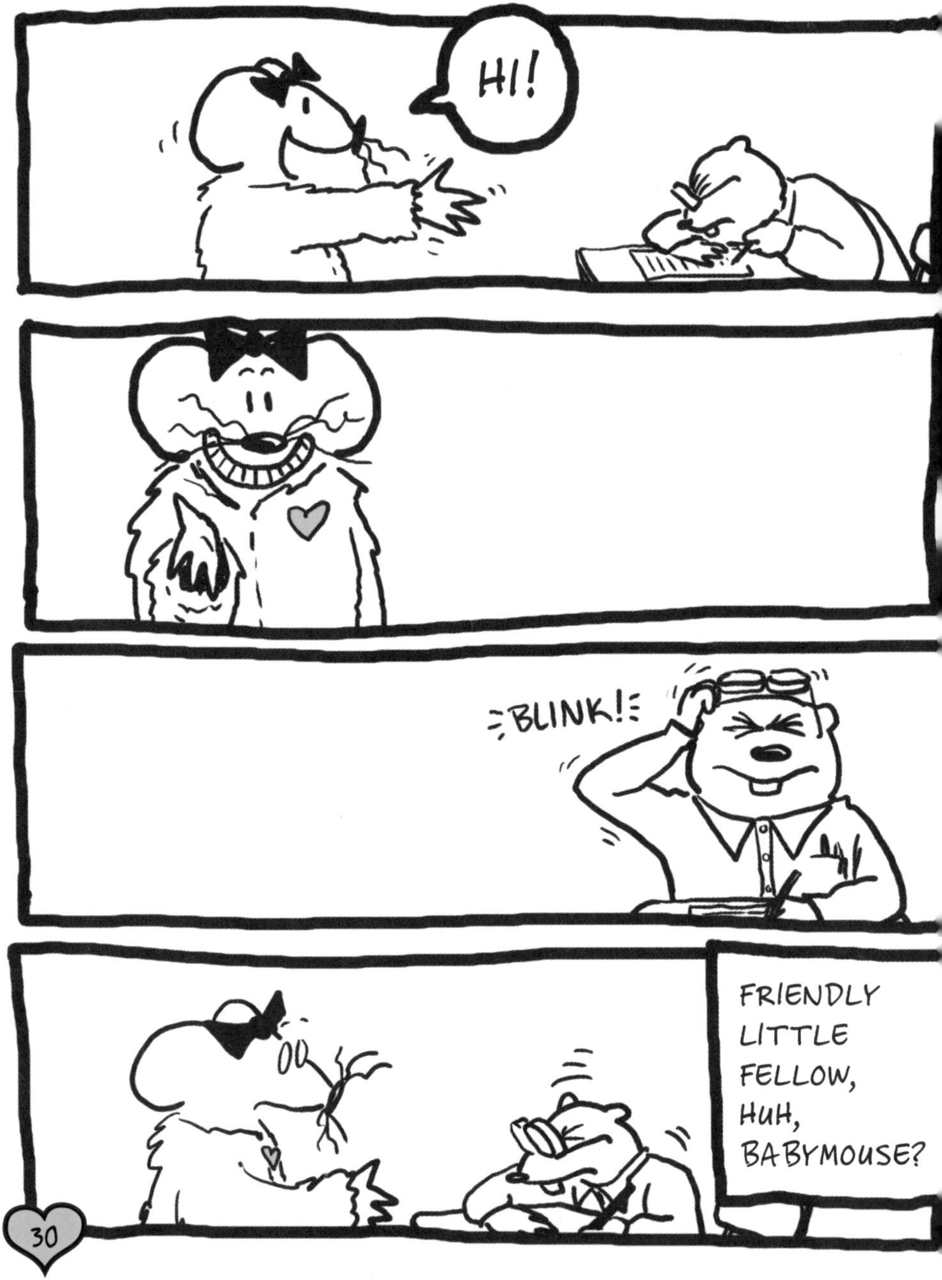
HI!
BLINK!
FRIENDLY LITTLE FELLOW, HUH, BABYMOUSE?

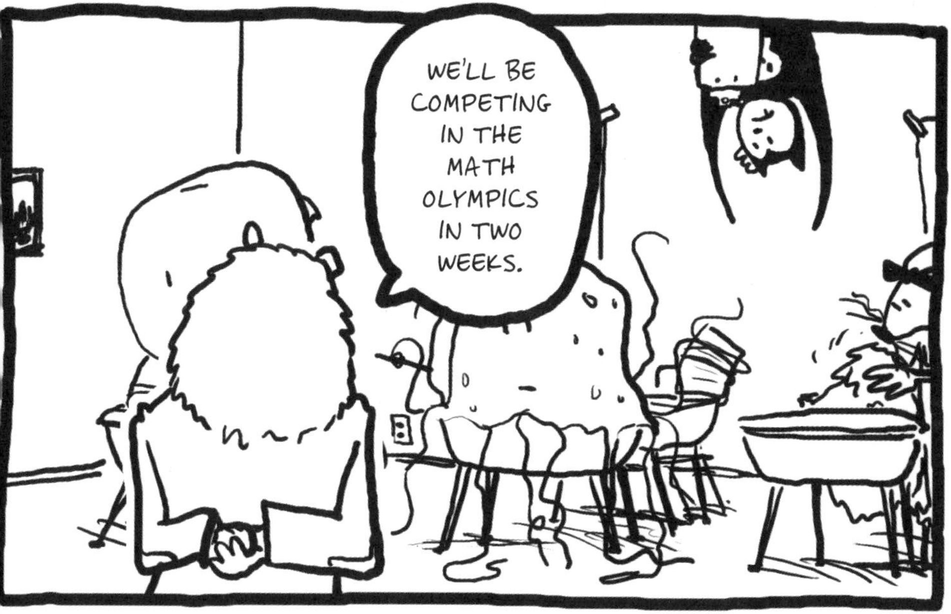
WE'LL BE COMPETING IN THE MATH OLYMPICS IN TWO WEEKS.

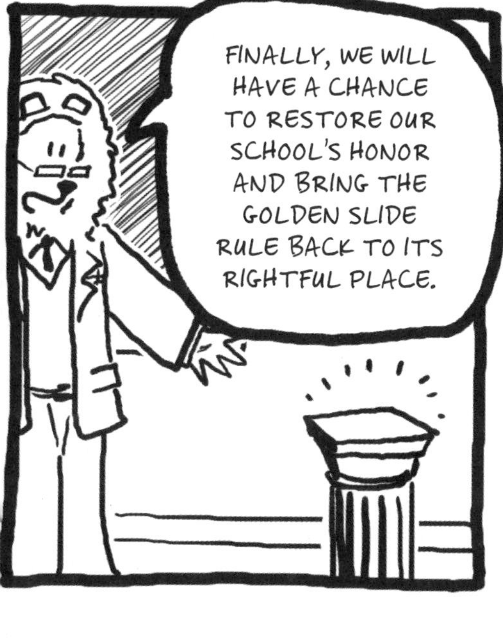
FINALLY, WE WILL HAVE A CHANCE TO RESTORE OUR SCHOOL'S HONOR AND BRING THE GOLDEN SLIDE RULE BACK TO ITS RIGHTFUL PLACE.

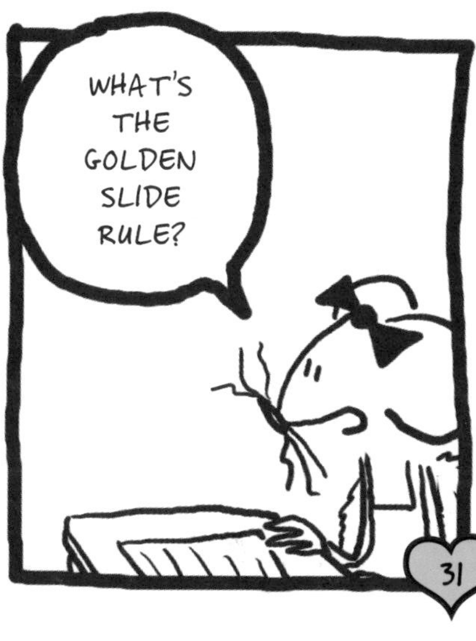
WHAT'S THE GOLDEN SLIDE RULE?

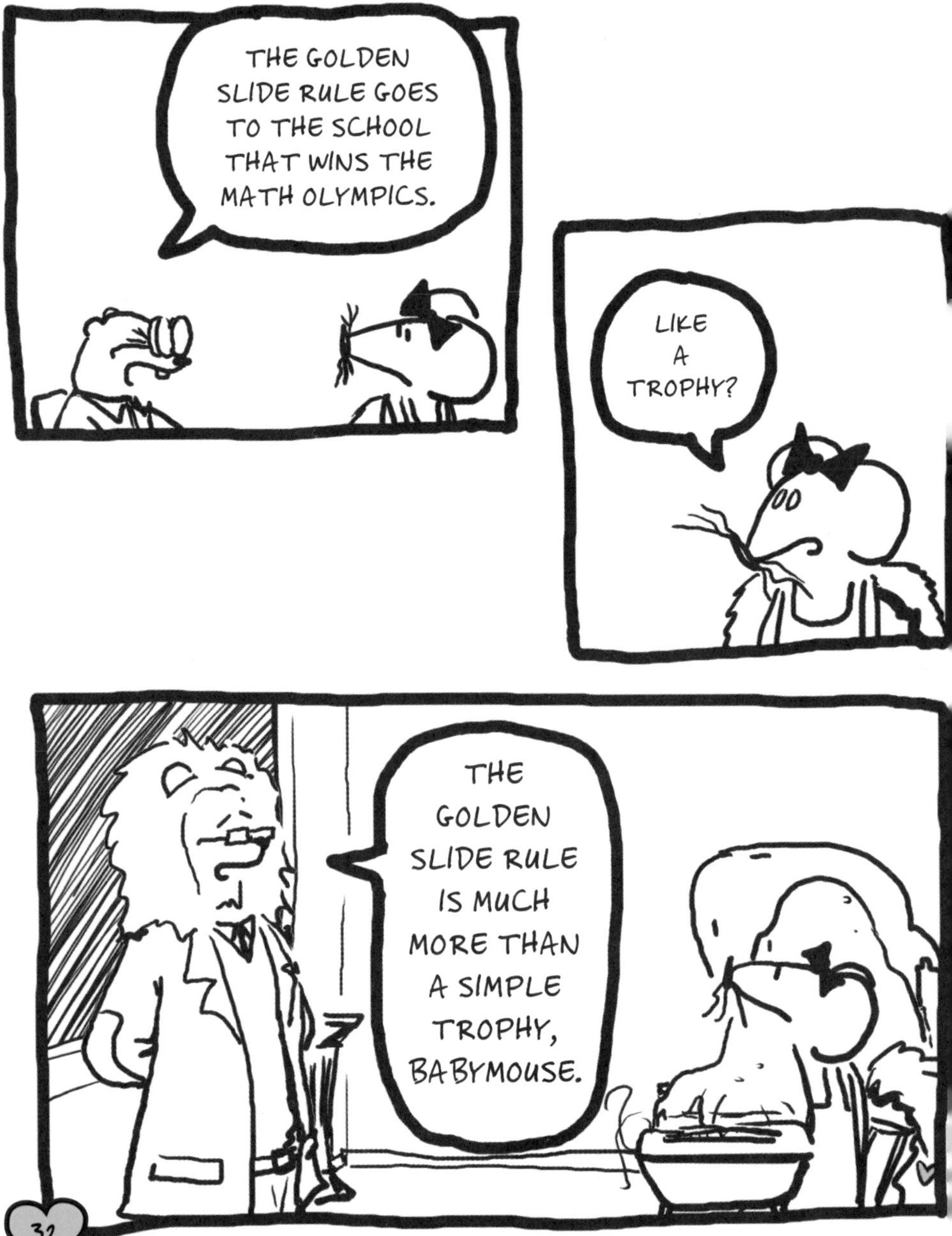
THE GOLDEN SLIDE RULE GOES TO THE SCHOOL THAT WINS THE MATH OLYMPICS.
LIKE A TROPHY?
THE GOLDEN SLIDE RULE IS MUCH MORE THAN A SIMPLE TROPHY, BABYMOUSE.

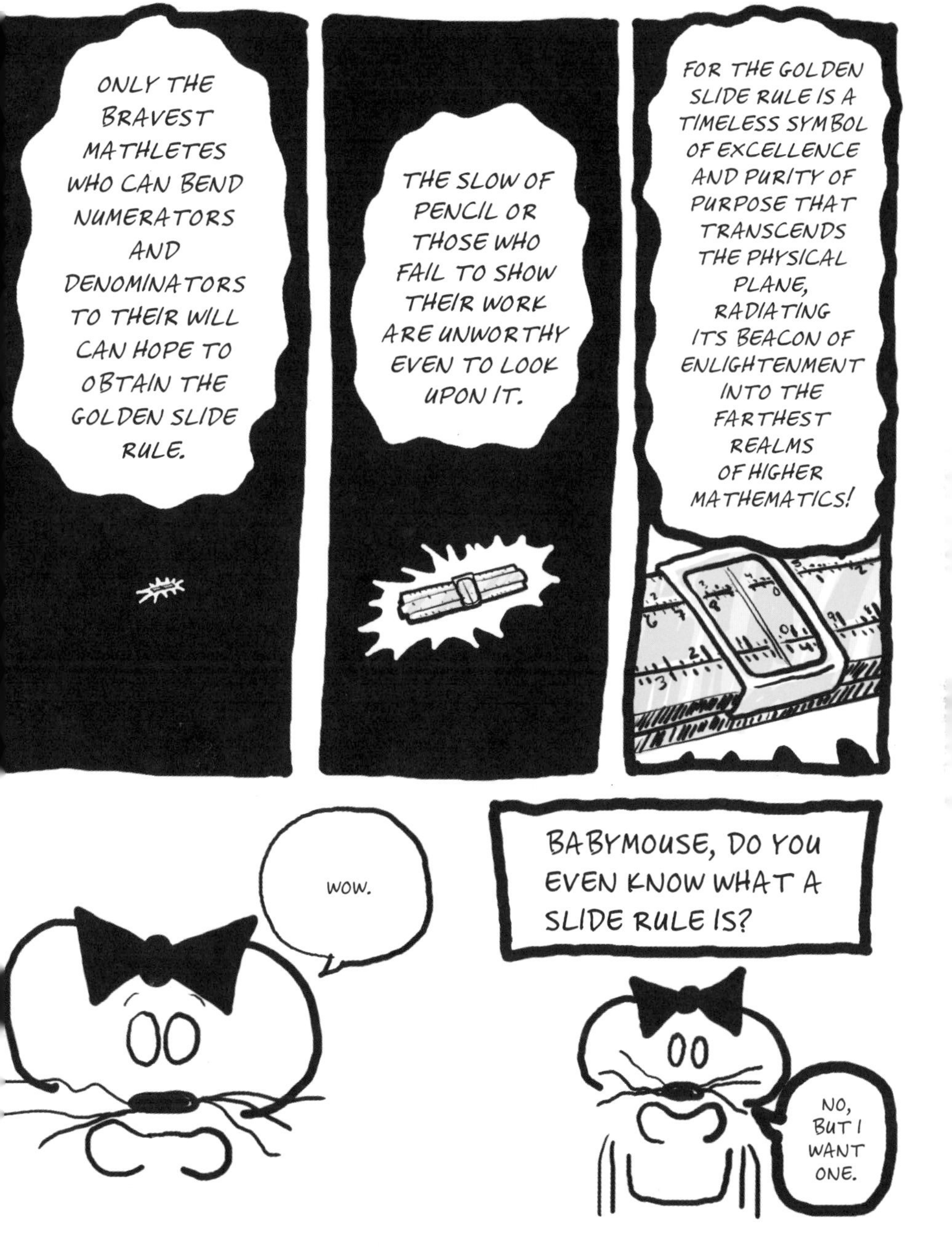
ONLY THE BRAVEST MATHLETES WHO CAN BEND NUMERATORS AND DENOMINATORS TO THEIR WILL CAN HOPE TO OBTAIN THE GOLDEN SLIDE RULE.
THE SLOW OF PENCIL OR THOSE WHO FAIL TO SHOW THEIR WORK ARE UNWORTHY EVEN TO LOOK UPON IT.
FOR THE GOLDEN SLIDE RULE IS A TIMELESS SYMBOL OF EXCELLENCE AND PURITY OF PURPOSE THAT TRANSCENDS THE PHYSICAL PLANE, RADIATING ITS BEACON OF ENLIGHTENMENT INTO THE FARTHEST REALMS OF HIGHER MATHEMATICS!
WOW.
BABYMOUSE, DO YOU EVEN KNOW WHAT A SLIDE RULE IS?
NO, BUT I WANT ONE.

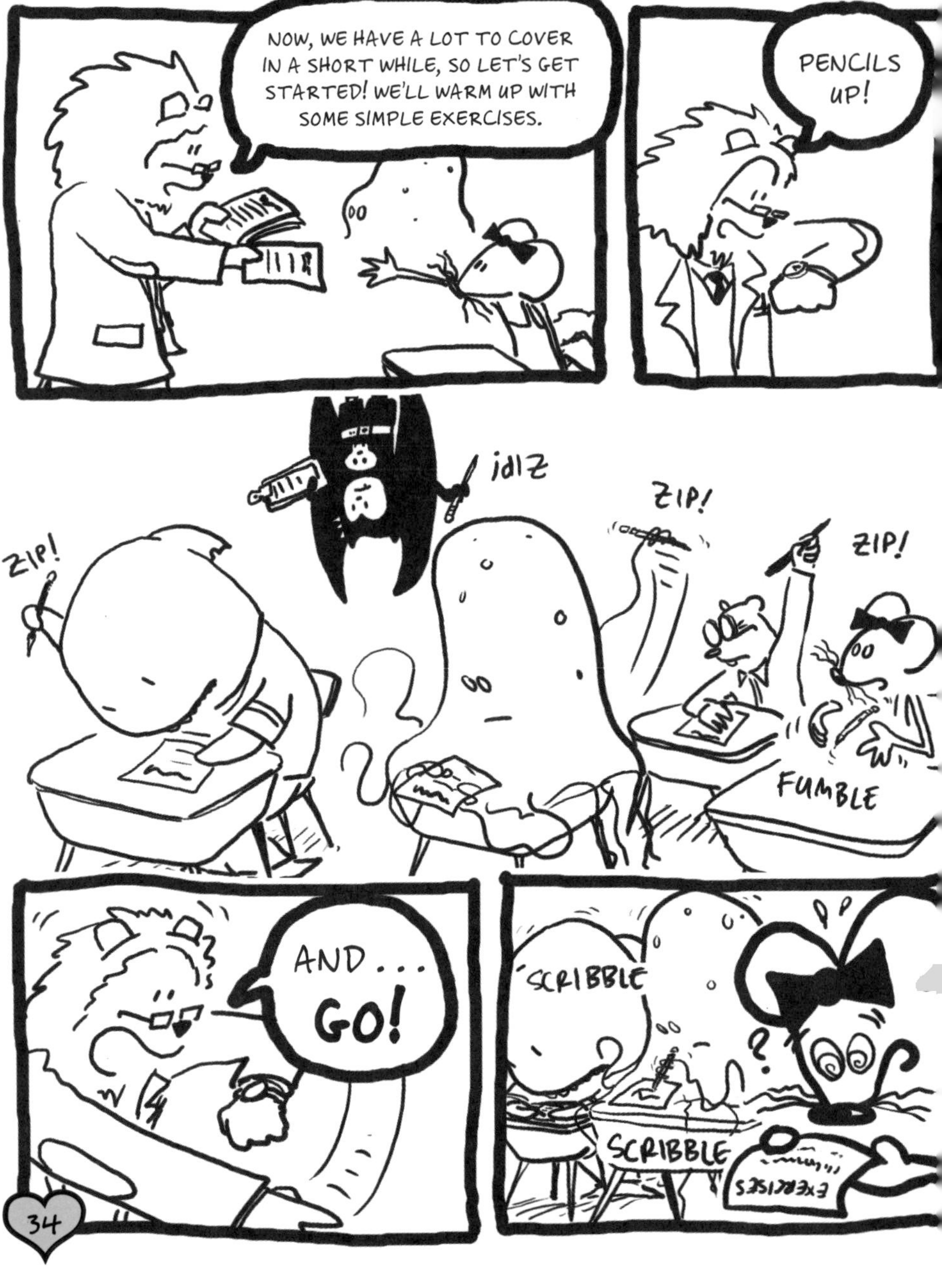
NOW, WE HAVE A LOT TO COVER IN A SHORT WHILE, SO LET'S GET STARTED! WE'LL WARM UP WITH SOME SIMPLE EXERCISES.
PENCILS UP!
ZIP!
ZIP!
ZIP!
ZIP!
FUMBLE
AND....
GO!
SCRIBBLE
SCRIBBLE
EXERCISES

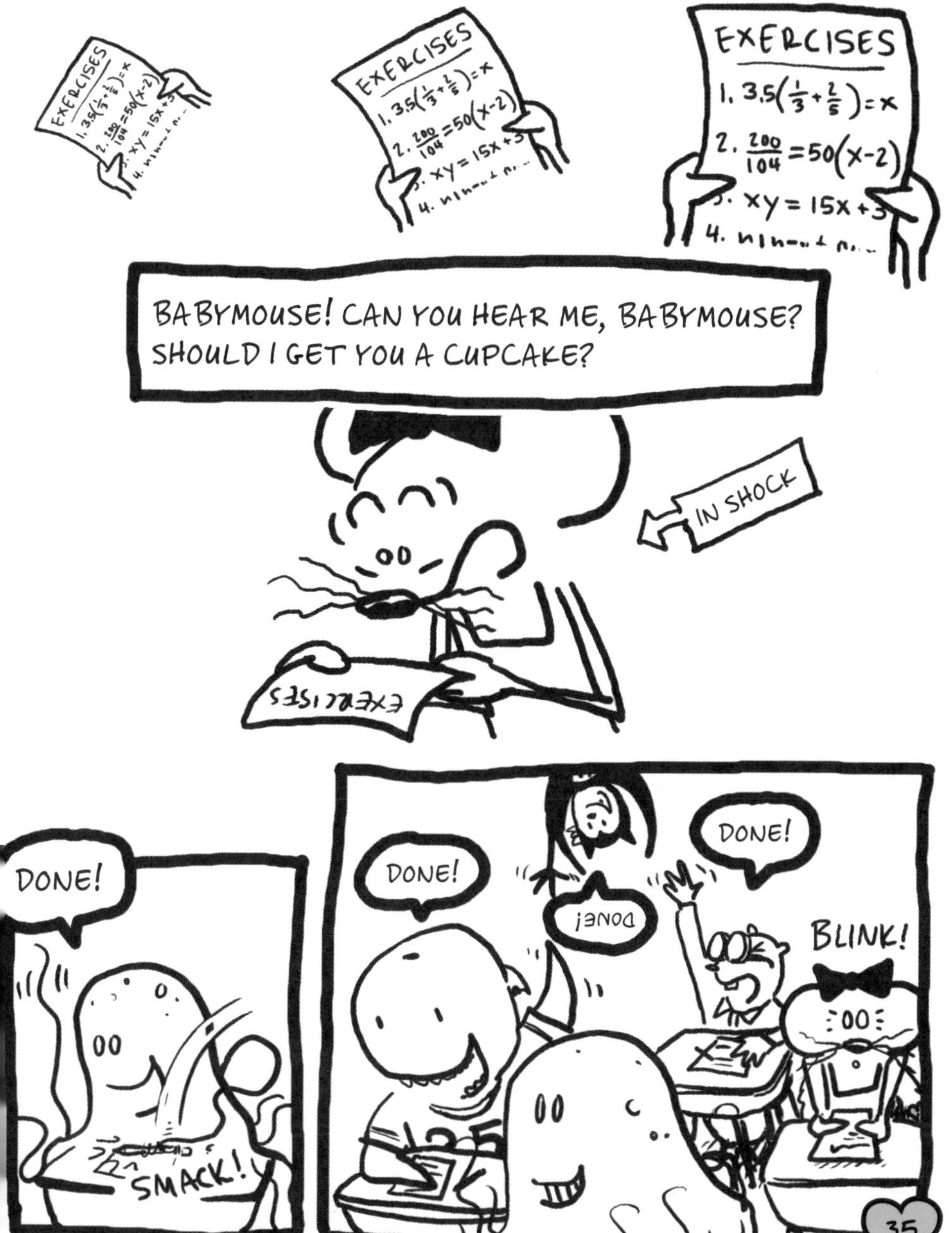
EXERCISES
1. 3.5(1/3 + 2/5) = x
2. 200/104 = 50(x-2)
3. xy = 15x + 3
4.
BABYMOUSE! CAN YOU HEAR ME, BABYMOUSE? SHOULD I GET YOU A CUPCAKE?
IN SHOCK
EXERCISES
DONE!
SMACK!
DONE!
DONE!
DONE!
BLINK!

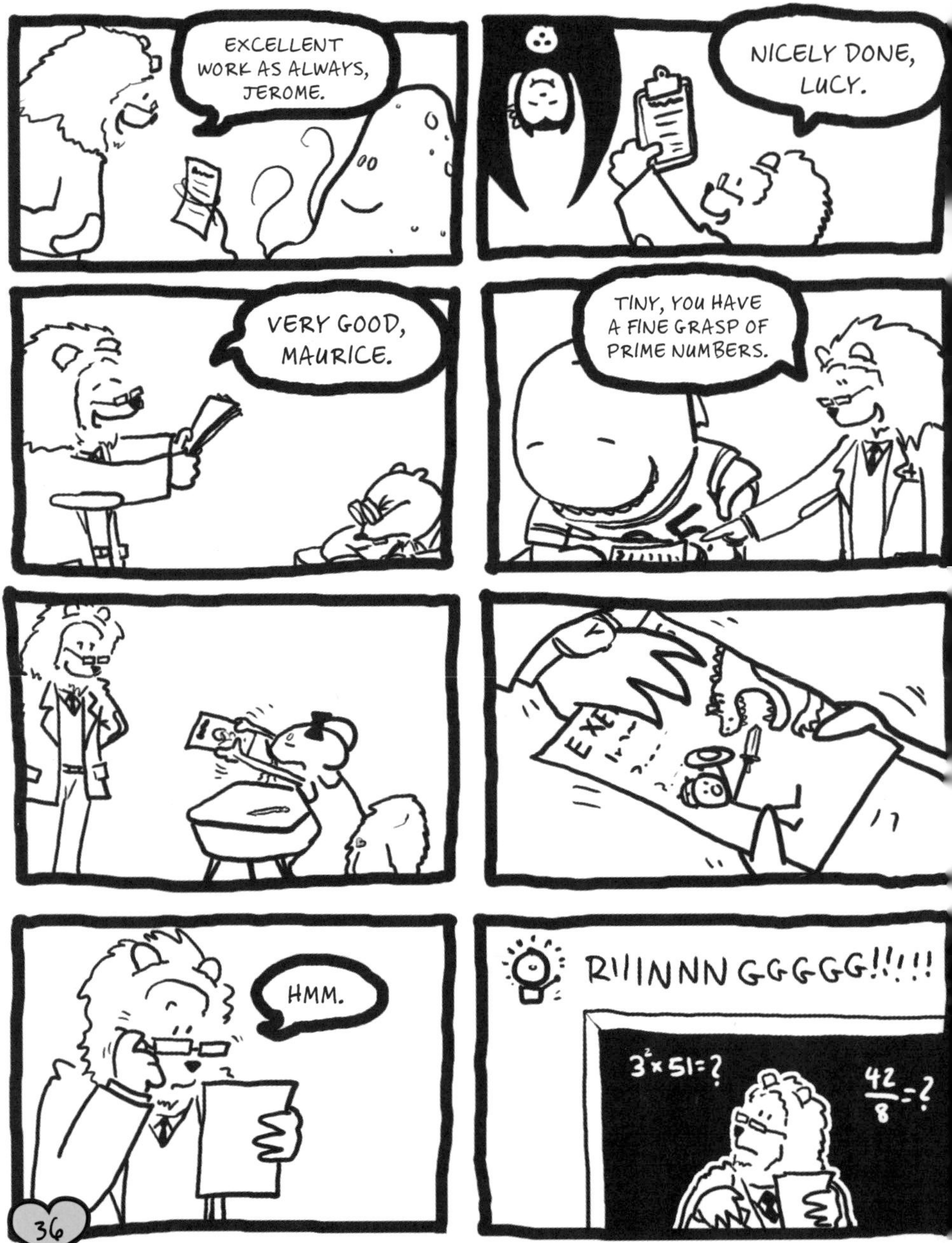
EXCELLENT WORK AS ALWAYS, JEROME.
NICELY DONE, LUCY.
VERY GOOD, MAURICE.
TINY, YOU HAVE A FINE GRASP OF PRIME NUMBERS.
HMM.
RIIINNNGGGGG!!!!!
3²×51=?
42/8=?

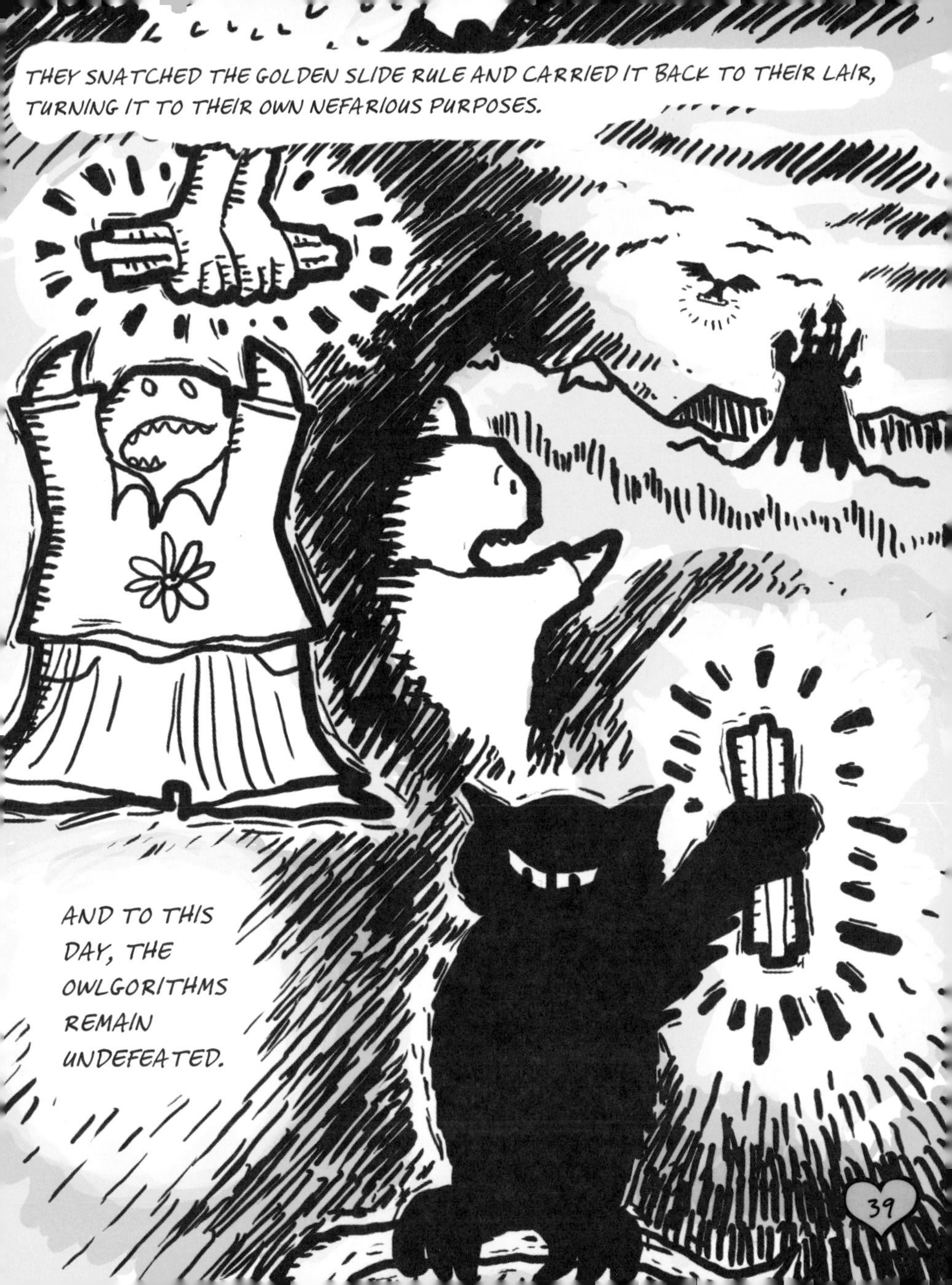
THEY SNATCHED THE GOLDEN SLIDE RULE AND CARRIED IT BACK TO THEIR LAIR, TURNING IT TO THEIR OWN NEFARIOUS PURPOSES.
AND TO THIS DAY, THE OWLGORITHMS REMAIN UNDEFEATED.

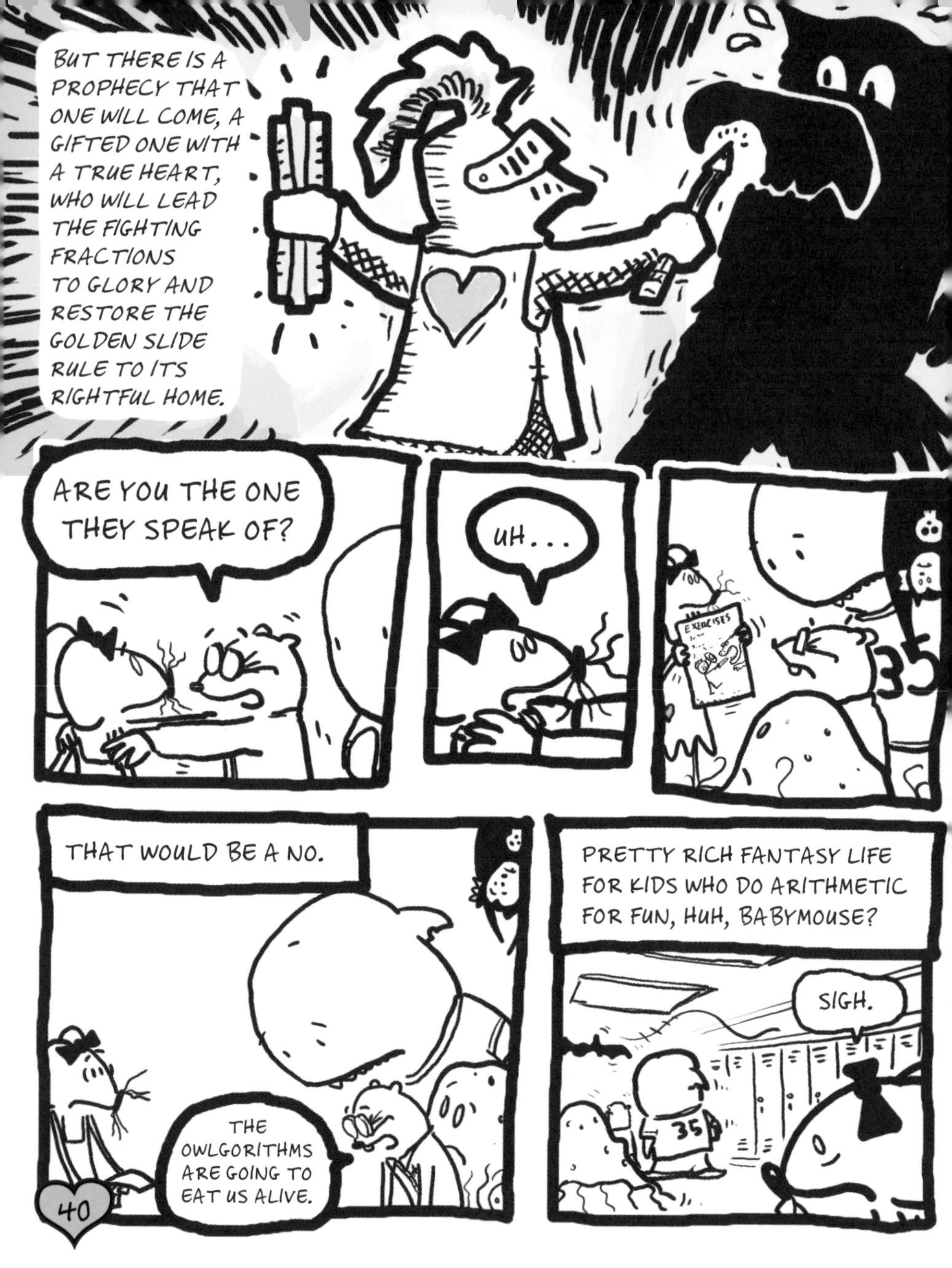
BUT THERE IS A PROPHECY THAT ONE WILL COME, A GIFTED ONE WITH A TRUE HEART, WHO WILL LEAD THE FIGHTING FRACTIONS TO GLORY AND RESTORE THE GOLDEN SLIDE RULE TO ITS RIGHTFUL HOME.
ARE YOU THE ONE THEY SPEAK OF?
UH . . .
EXERCISES
35
THAT WOULD BE A NO.
THE OWLGORITHMS ARE GOING TO EAT US ALIVE.
PRETTY RICH FANTASY LIFE FOR KIDS WHO DO ARITHMETIC FOR FUN, HUH, BABYMOUSE?
SIGH.
35

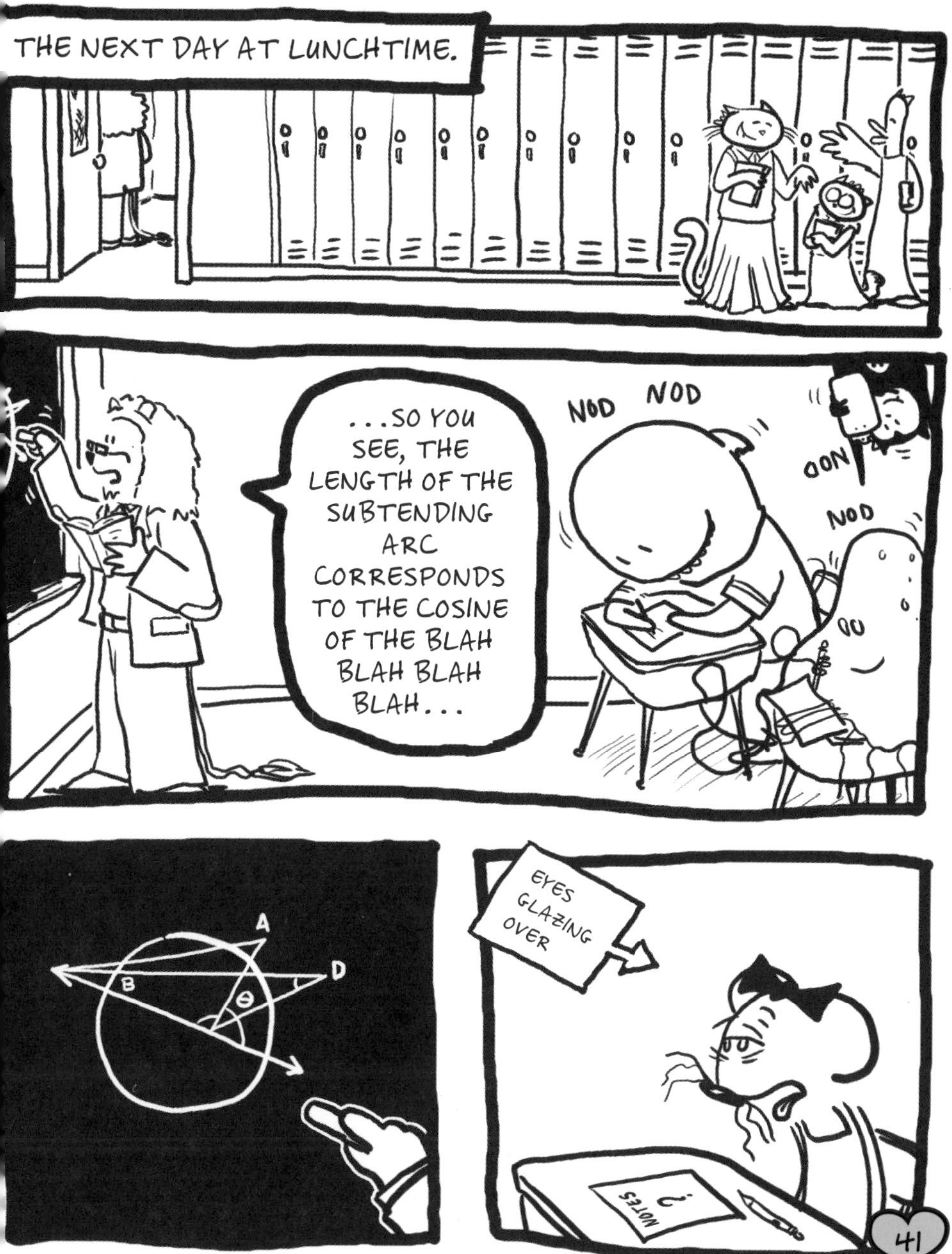
THE NEXT DAY AT LUNCHTIME.
...SO YOU SEE, THE LENGTH OF THE SUBTENDING ARC CORRESPONDS TO THE COSINE OF THE BLAH BLAH BLAH BLAH...
NOD
NOD
NOD
NOD
A
B
D
θ
EYES GLAZING OVER
NOTES
?

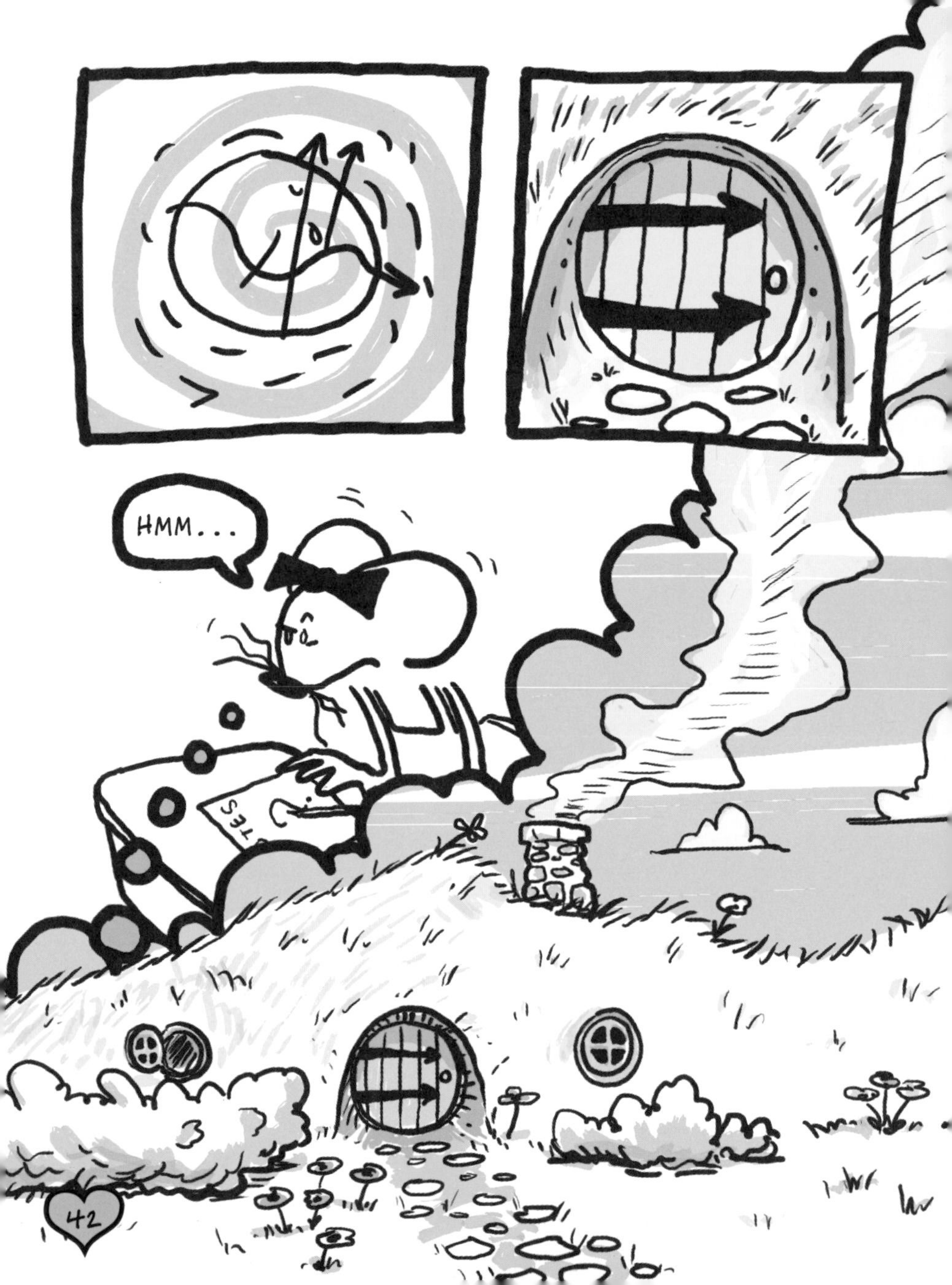
HMM...
TES

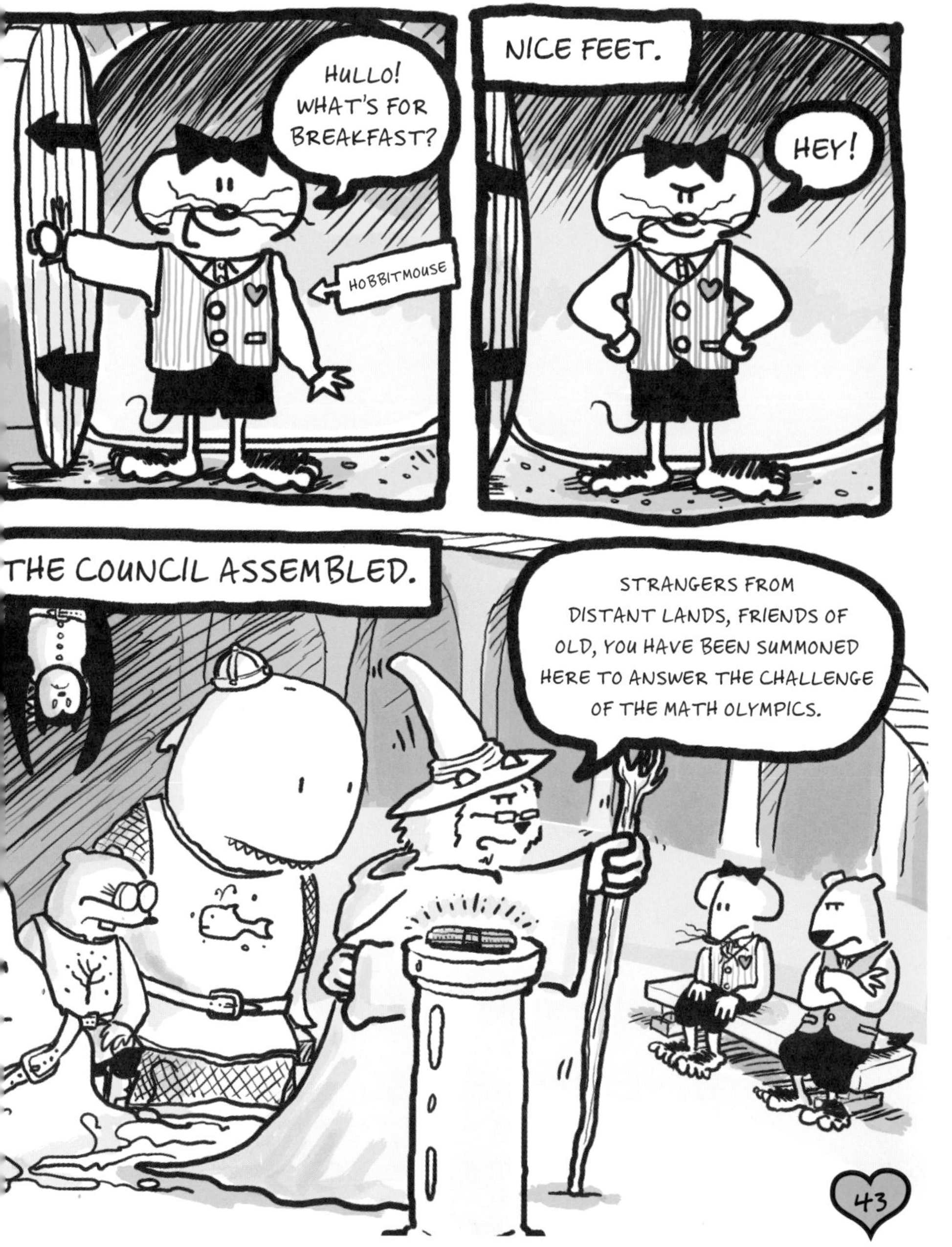
HULLO! WHAT'S FOR BREAKFAST?
HOBBITMOUSE
NICE FEET.
HEY!
THE COUNCIL ASSEMBLED.
STRANGERS FROM DISTANT LANDS, FRIENDS OF OLD, YOU HAVE BEEN SUMMONED HERE TO ANSWER THE CHALLENGE OF THE MATH OLYMPICS.

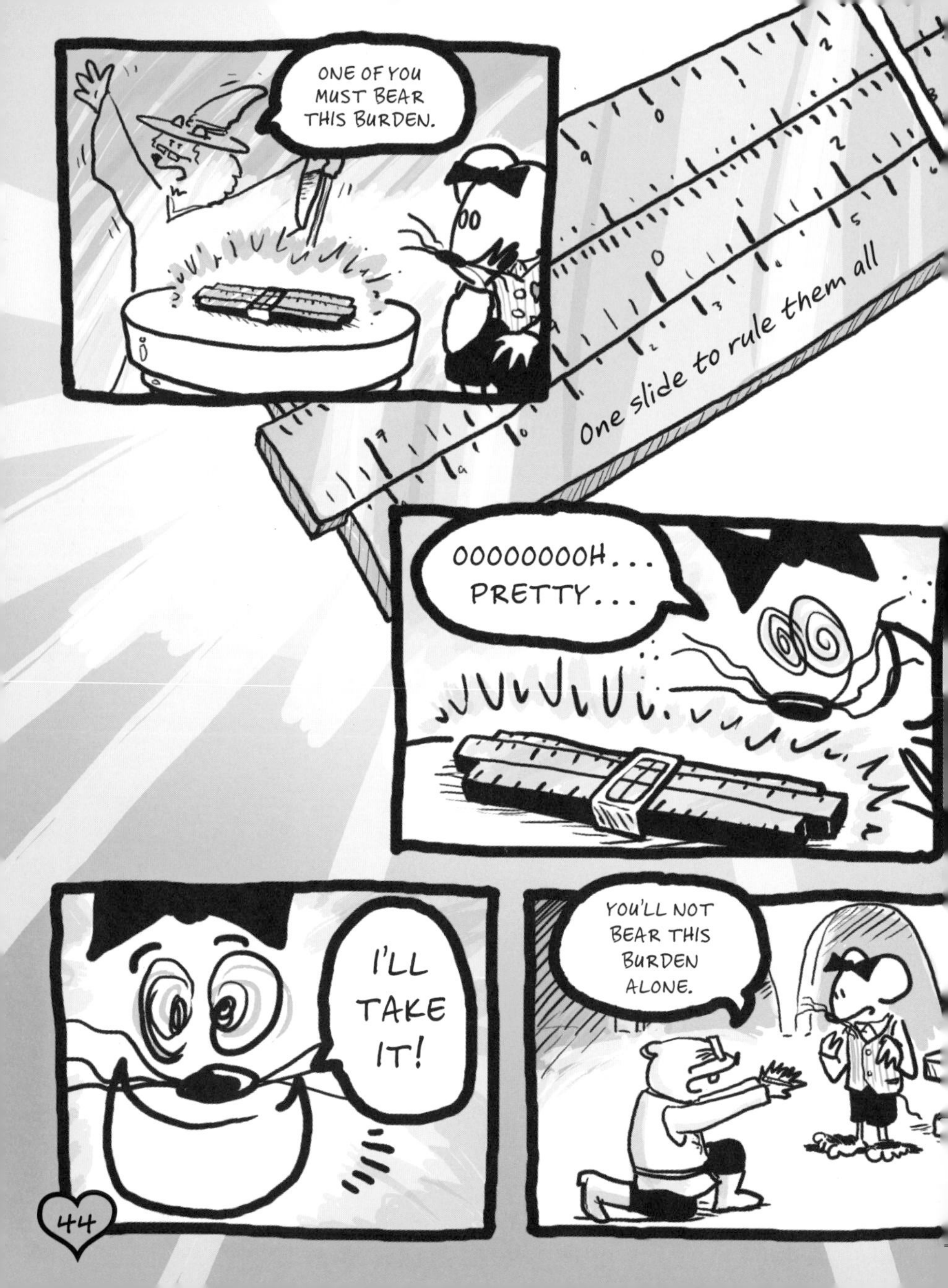
ONE OF YOU MUST BEAR THIS BURDEN.
One slide to rule them all
OOOOOOOOH... PRETTY...
I'LL TAKE IT!
YOU'LL NOT BEAR THIS BURDEN ALONE.

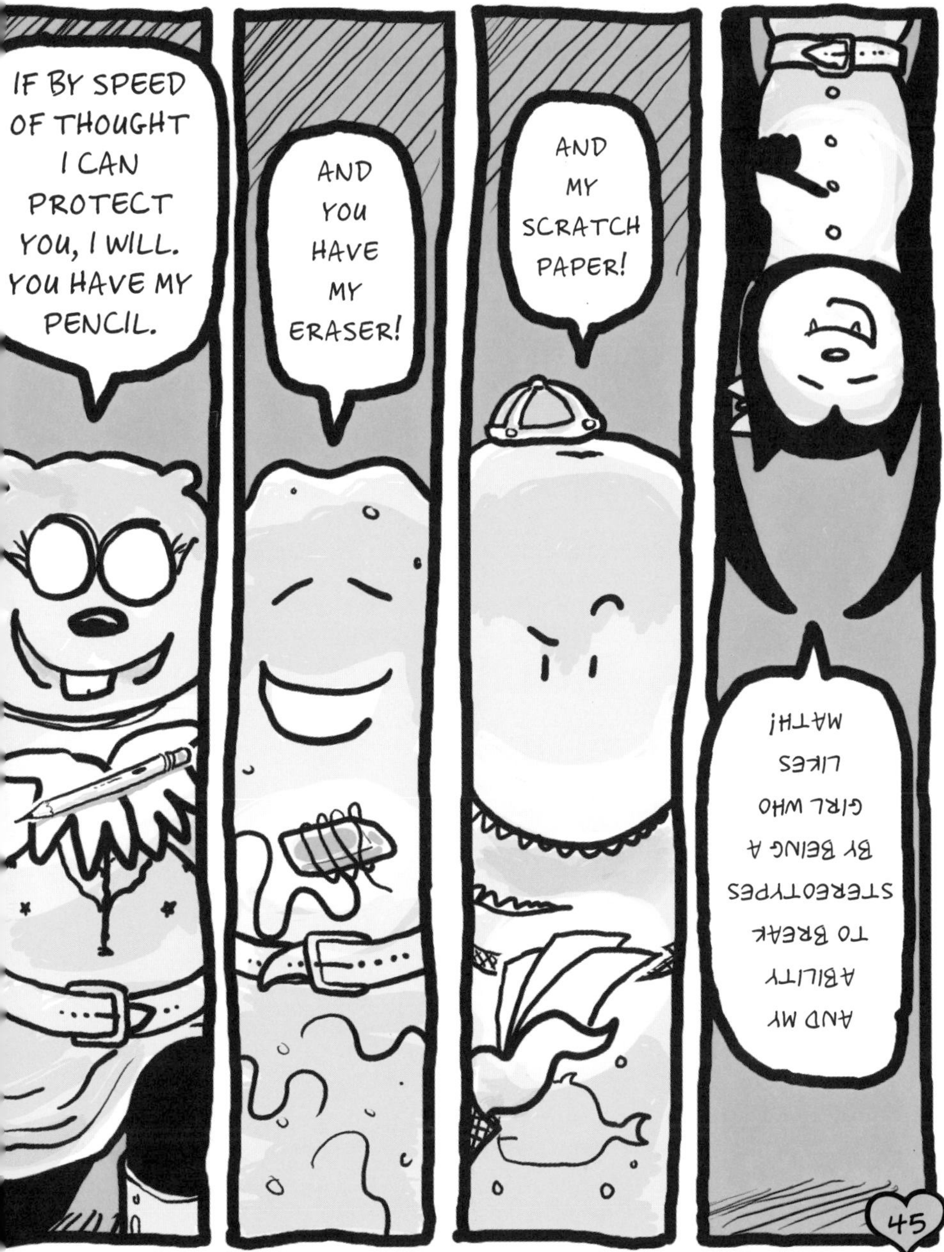
IF BY SPEED OF THOUGHT I CAN PROTECT YOU, I WILL. YOU HAVE MY PENCIL.
AND YOU HAVE MY ERASER!
AND MY SCRATCH PAPER!
AND MY ABILITY TO BREAK STEREOTYPES BY BEING A GIRL WHO LIKES MATH!

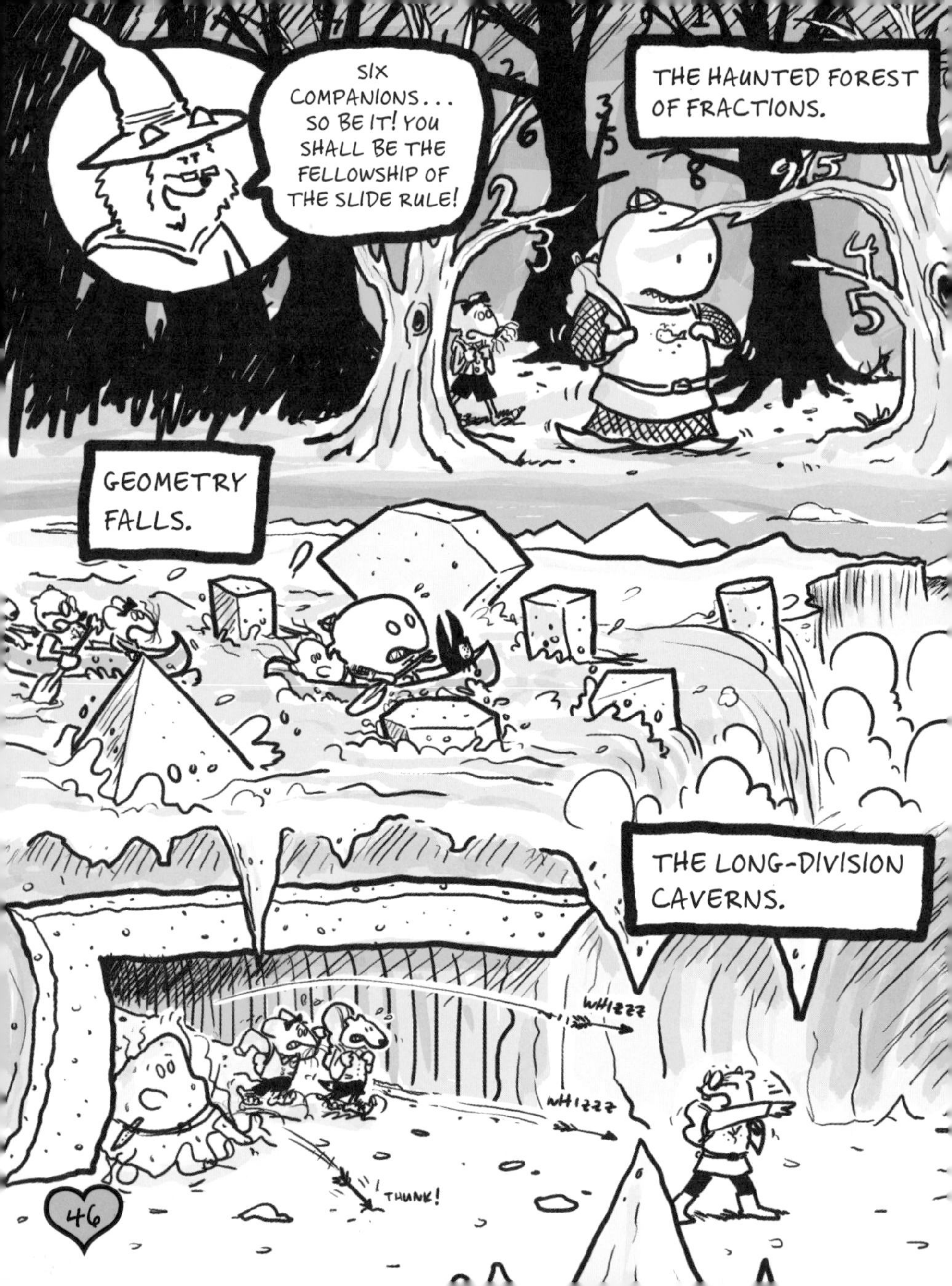

SIX COMPANIONS... SO BE IT! YOU SHALL BE THE FELLOWSHIP OF THE SLIDE RULE!
THE HAUNTED FOREST OF FRACTIONS.
GEOMETRY FALLS.
THE LONG-DIVISION CAVERNS.
WHIZZZ
WHIZZZ
THUNK!

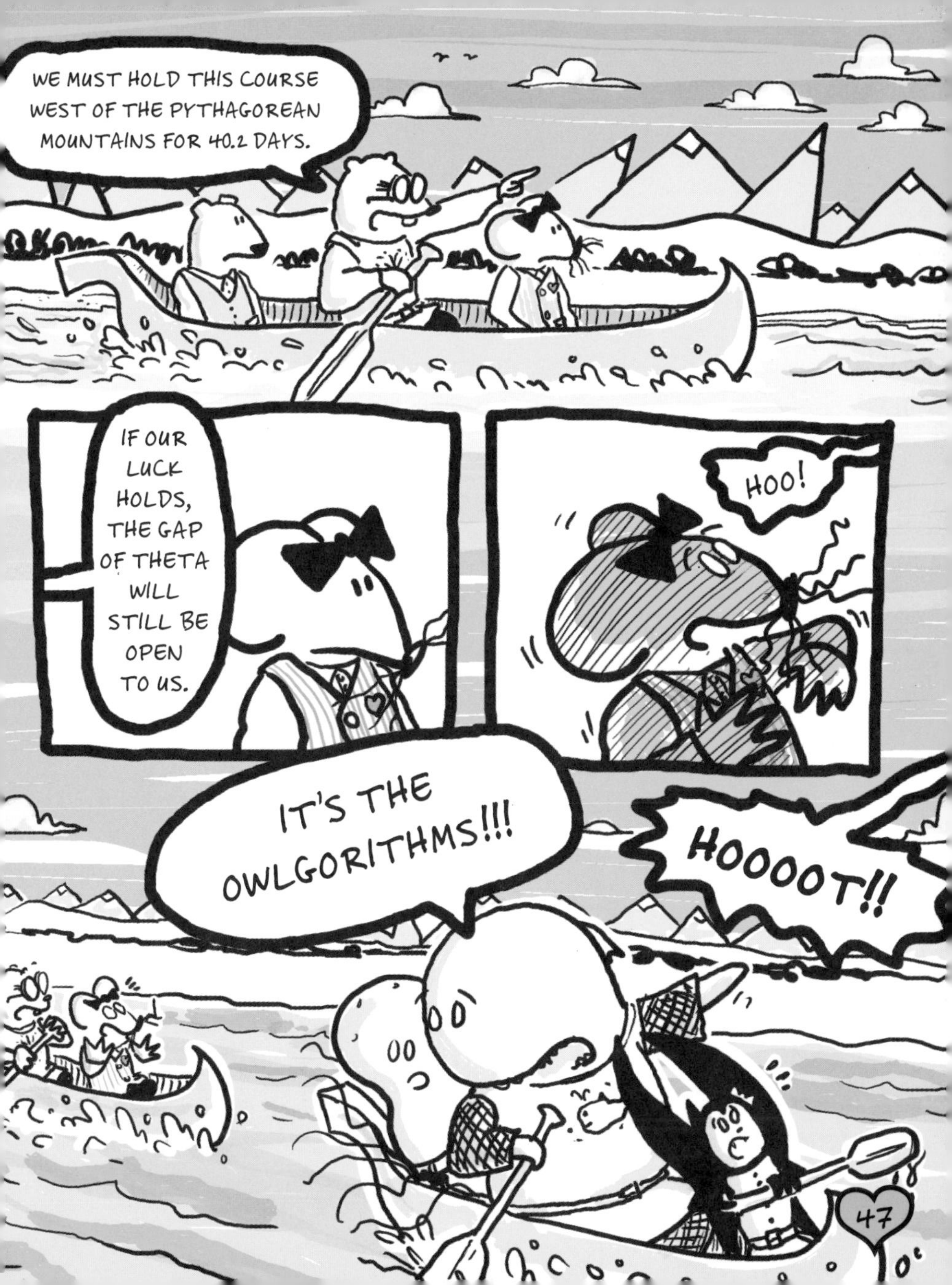
WE MUST HOLD THIS COURSE WEST OF THE PYTHAGOREAN MOUNTAINS FOR 40.2 DAYS.
IF OUR LUCK HOLDS, THE GAP OF THETA WILL STILL BE OPEN TO US.
HOO!
IT'S THE OWLGORITHMS!!!
HOOOOOT!!

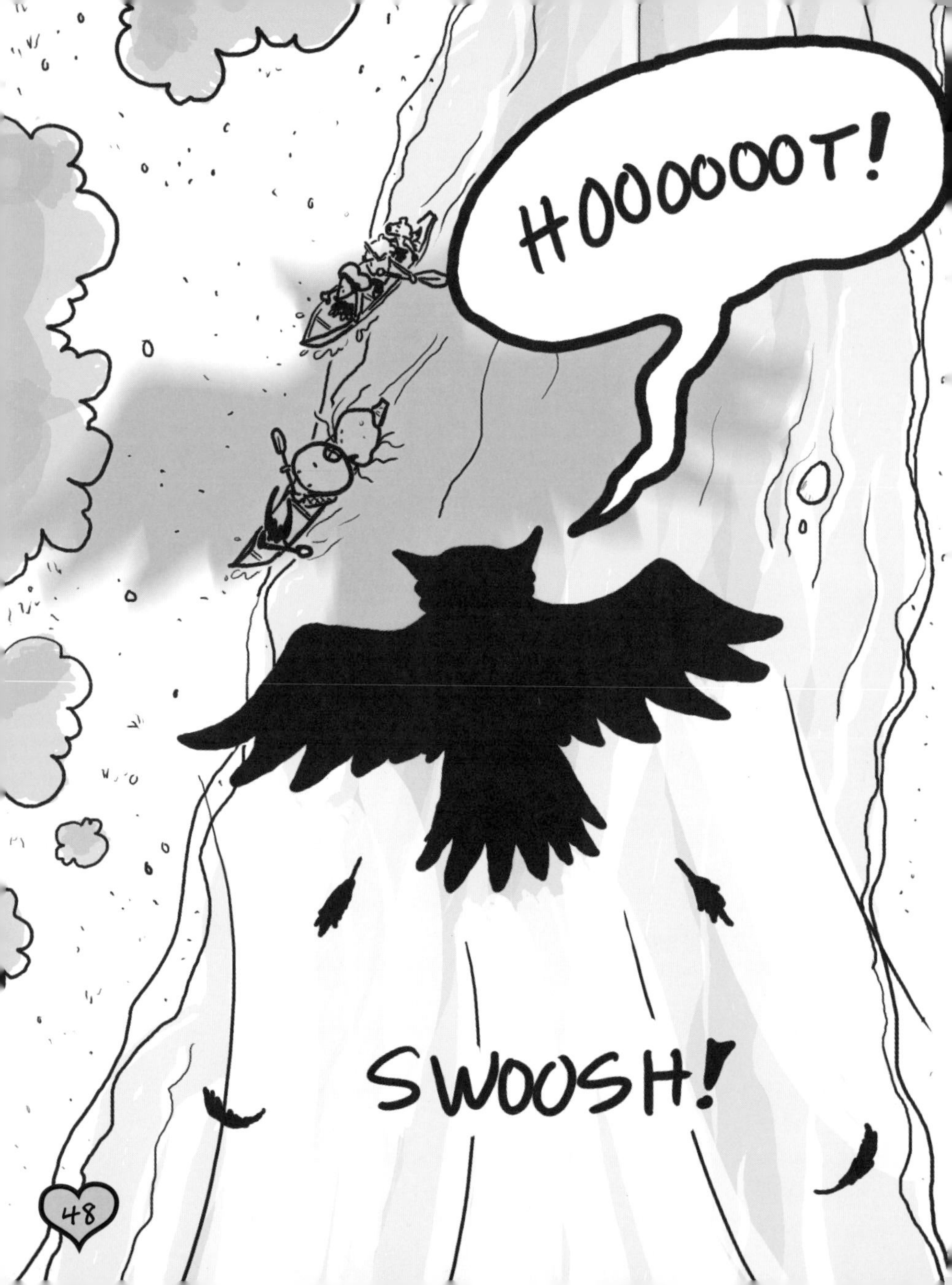
HOOOOOOT!
SWOOSH!

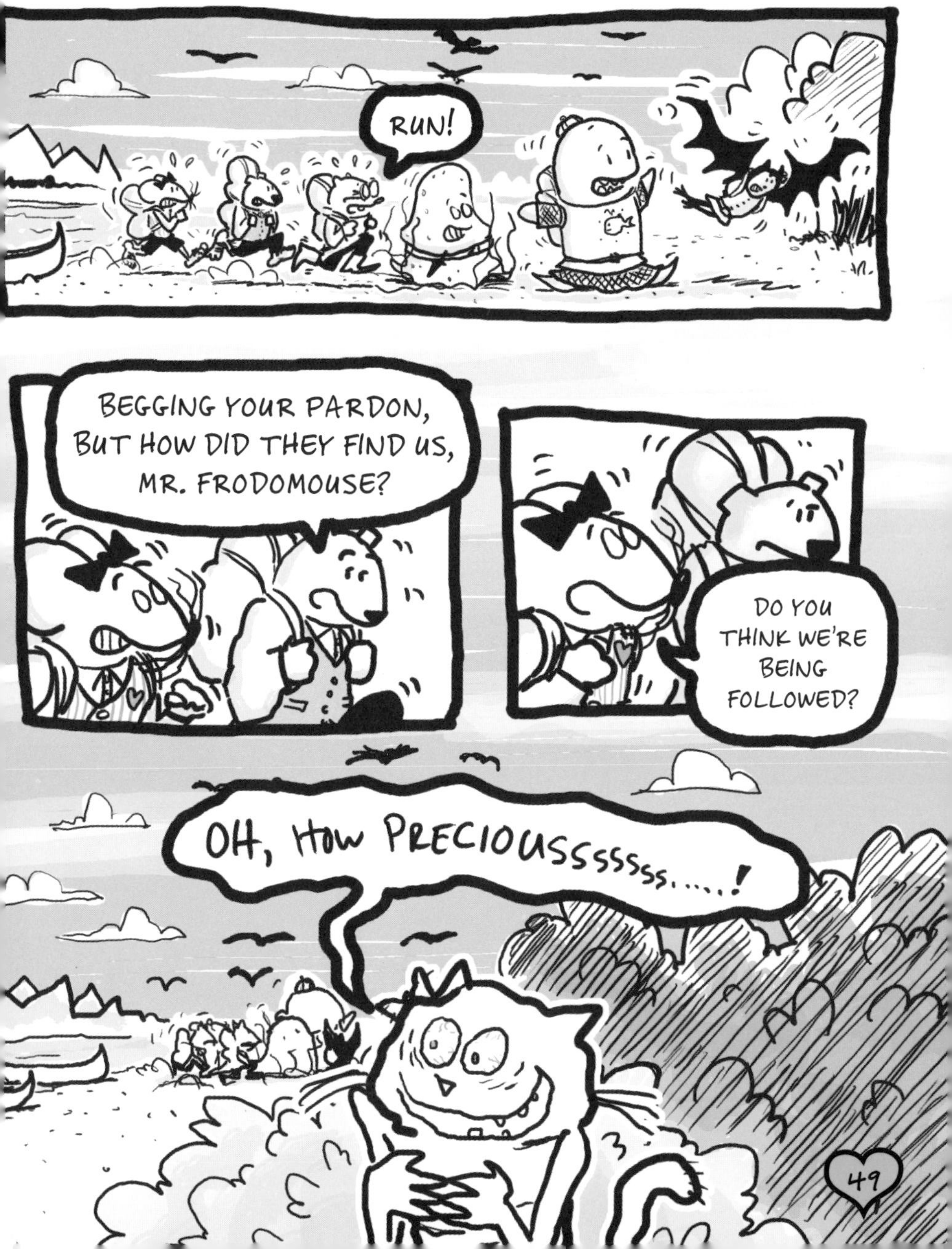
RUN!
BEGGING YOUR PARDON, BUT HOW DID THEY FIND US, MR. FRODOMOUSE?
DO YOU THINK WE'RE BEING FOLLOWED?
OH, HOW PRECIOUSSSSSSSS.....!

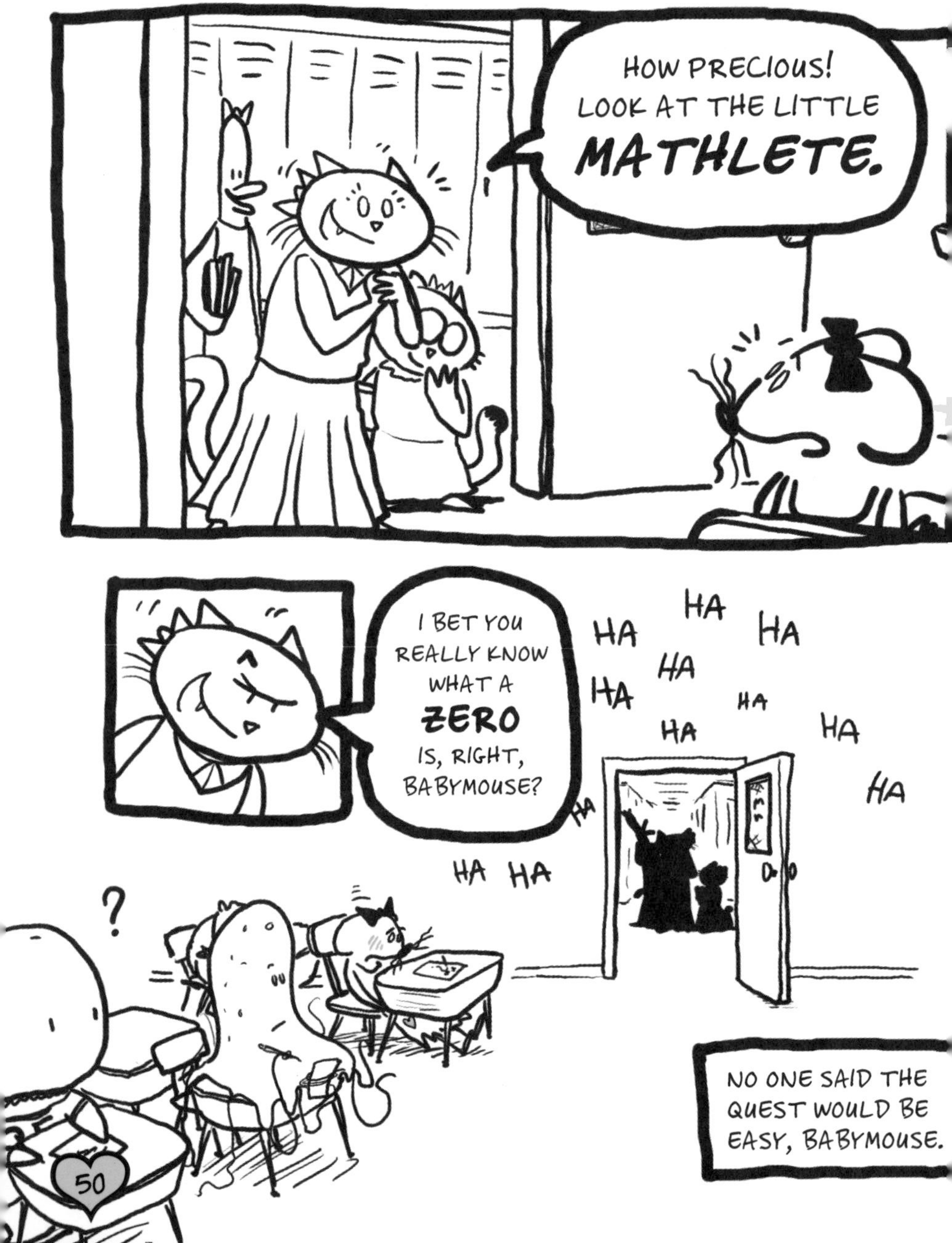
HOW PRECIOUS! LOOK AT THE LITTLE **MATHLETE.**
I BET YOU REALLY KNOW WHAT A **ZERO** IS, RIGHT, BABYMOUSE?
HA HA HA HA HA HA HA HA HA HA HA HA HA
?
NO ONE SAID THE QUEST WOULD BE EASY, BABYMOUSE.

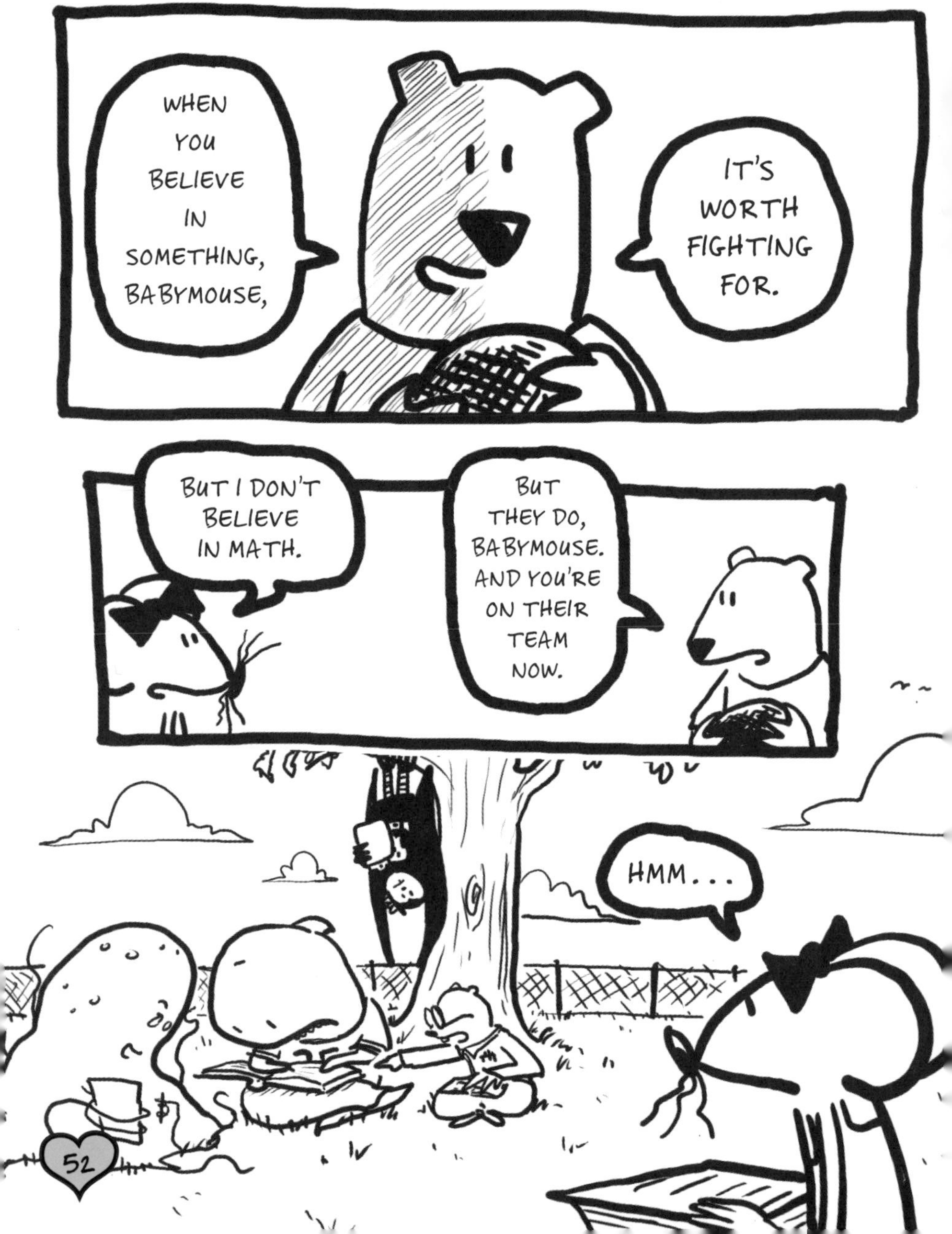
WHEN YOU BELIEVE IN SOMETHING, BABYMOUSE,
IT'S WORTH FIGHTING FOR.
BUT I DON'T BELIEVE IN MATH.
BUT THEY DO, BABYMOUSE. AND YOU'RE ON THEIR TEAM NOW.
HMM...

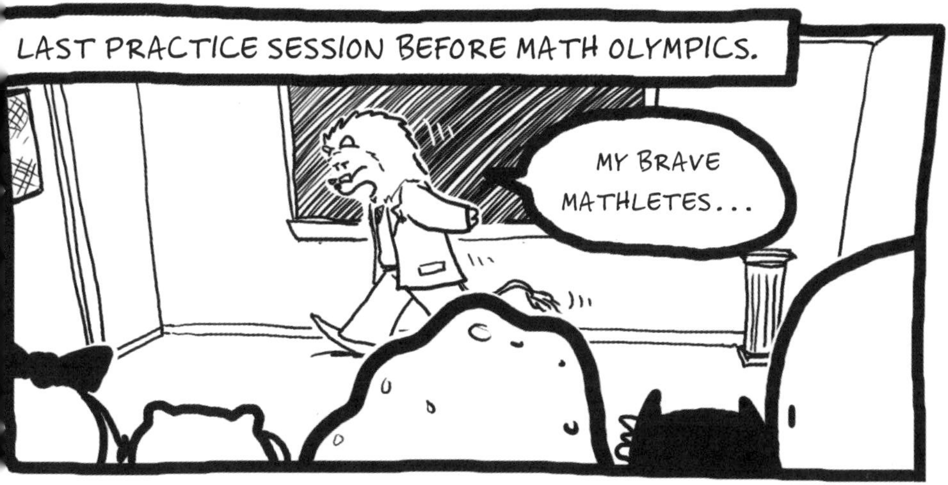
LAST PRACTICE SESSION BEFORE MATH OLYMPICS.
MY BRAVE MATHLETES...

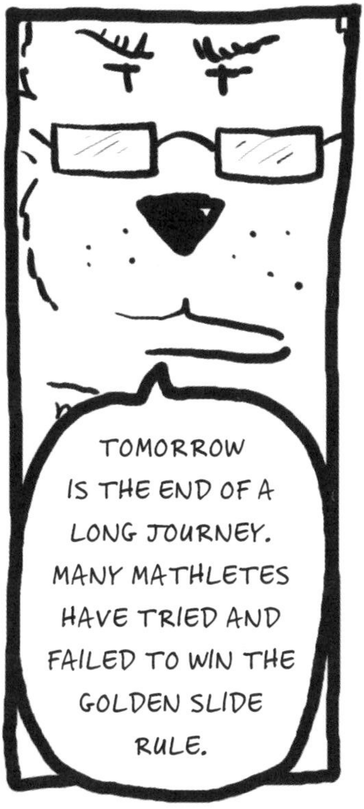
TOMORROW IS THE END OF A LONG JOURNEY. MANY MATHLETES HAVE TRIED AND FAILED TO WIN THE GOLDEN SLIDE RULE.

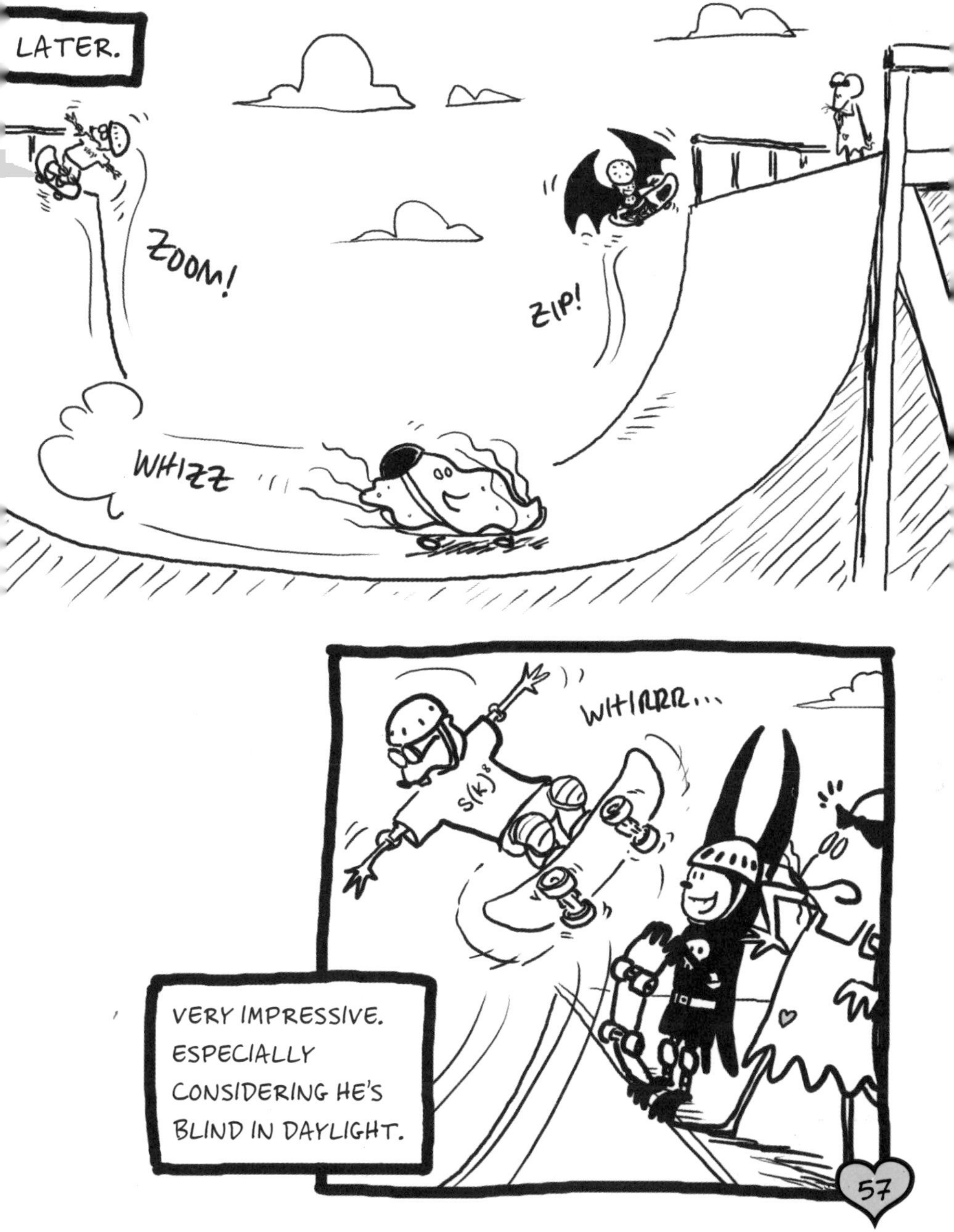
LATER.
ZOOM!
ZIP!
WHIZZ
WHIRRR...
VERY IMPRESSIVE. ESPECIALLY CONSIDERING HE'S BLIND IN DAYLIGHT.

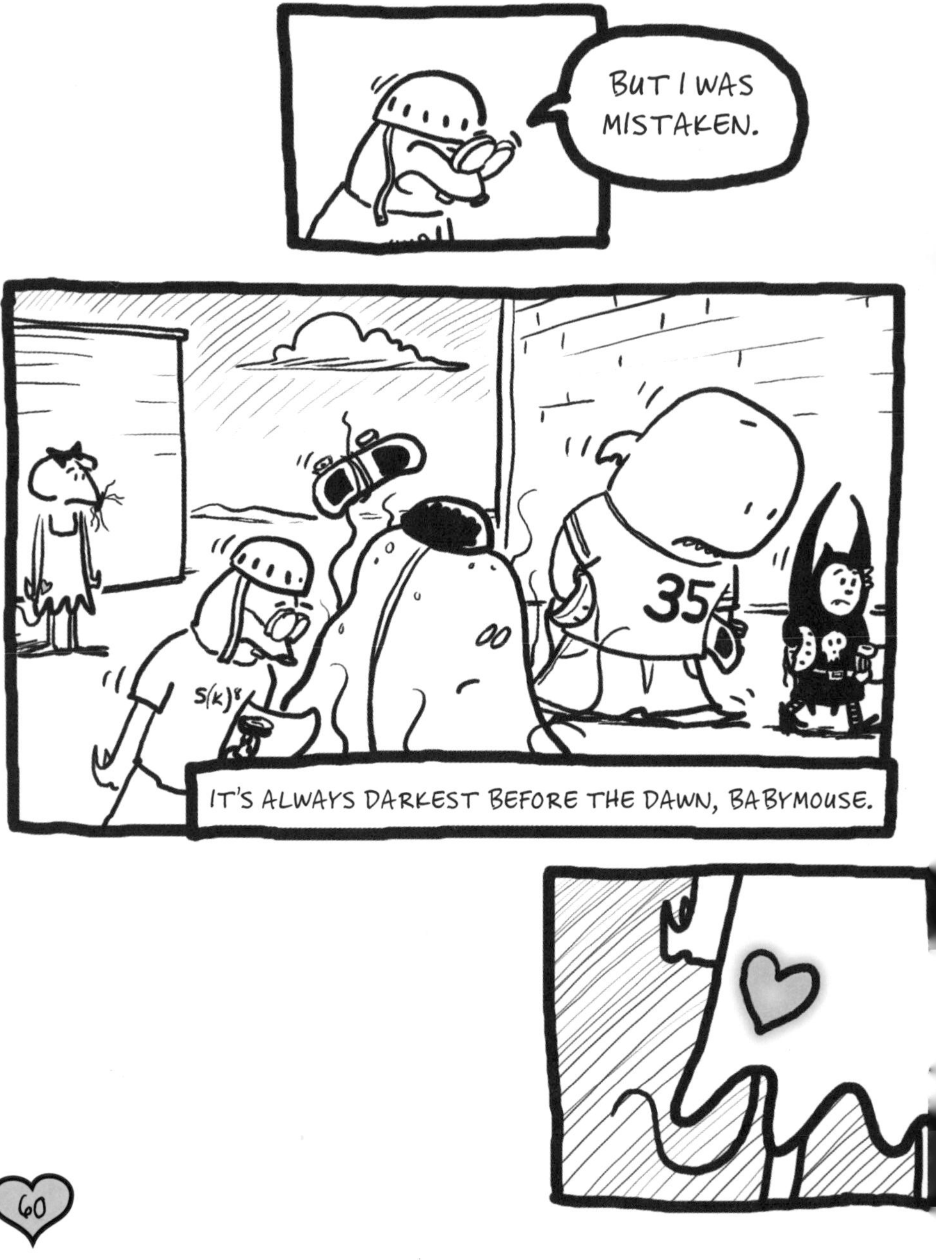
BUT I WAS MISTAKEN.
S(K)8
35
IT'S ALWAYS DARKEST BEFORE THE DAWN, BABYMOUSE.

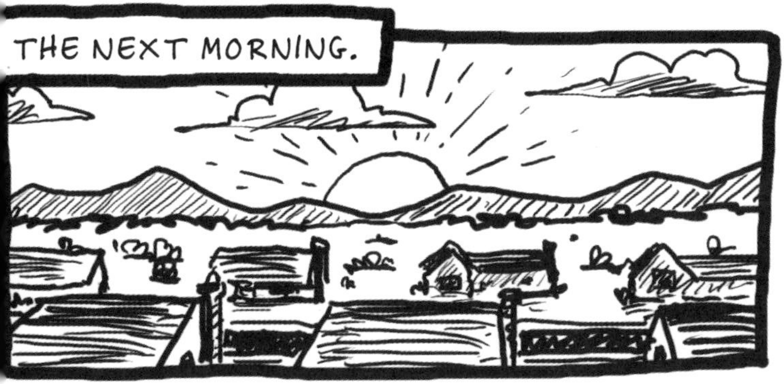
THE NEXT MORNING.

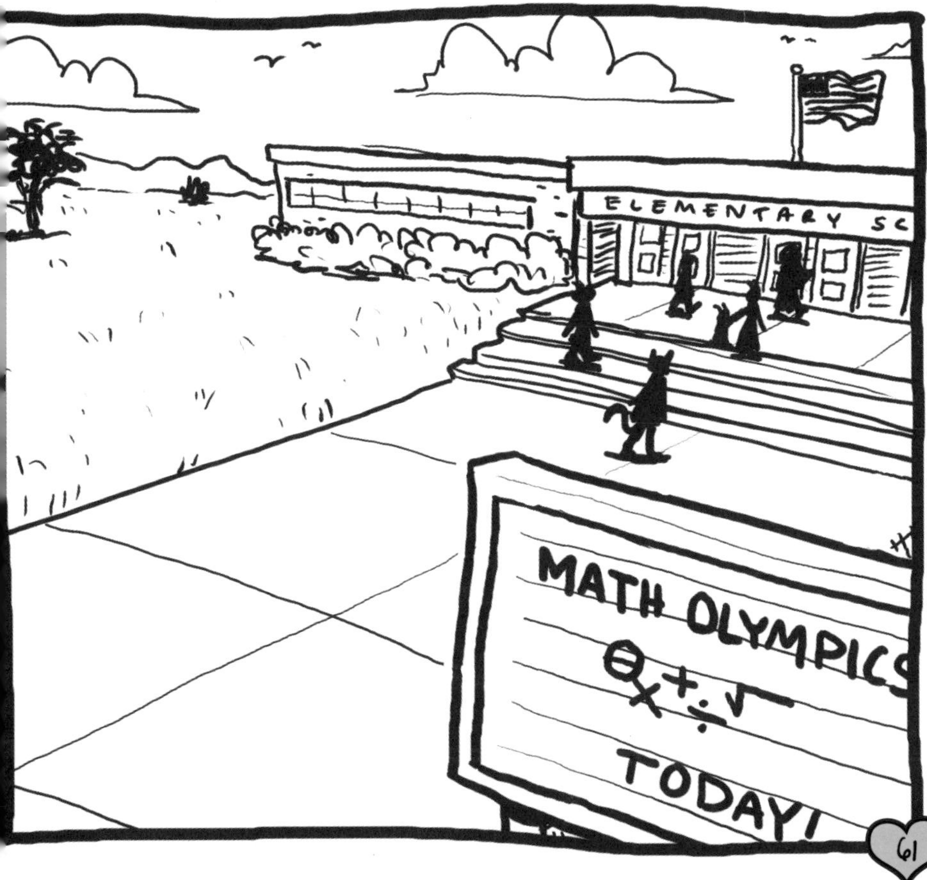
ELEMENTARY SC
MATH OLYMPICS
TODAY!

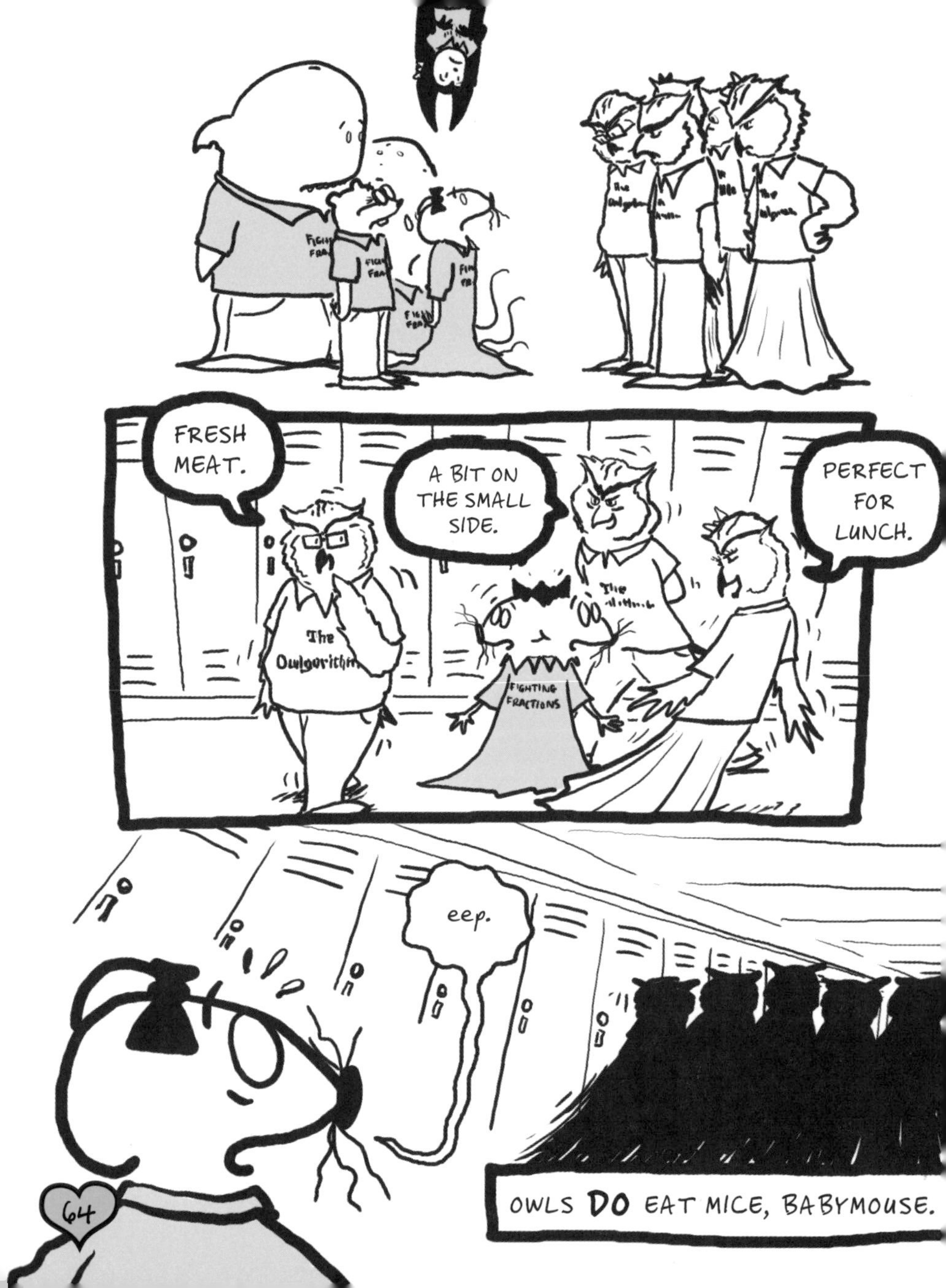

FRESH MEAT.
A BIT ON THE SMALL SIDE.
PERFECT FOR LUNCH.
eep.
OWLS **DO** EAT MICE, BABYMOUSE.

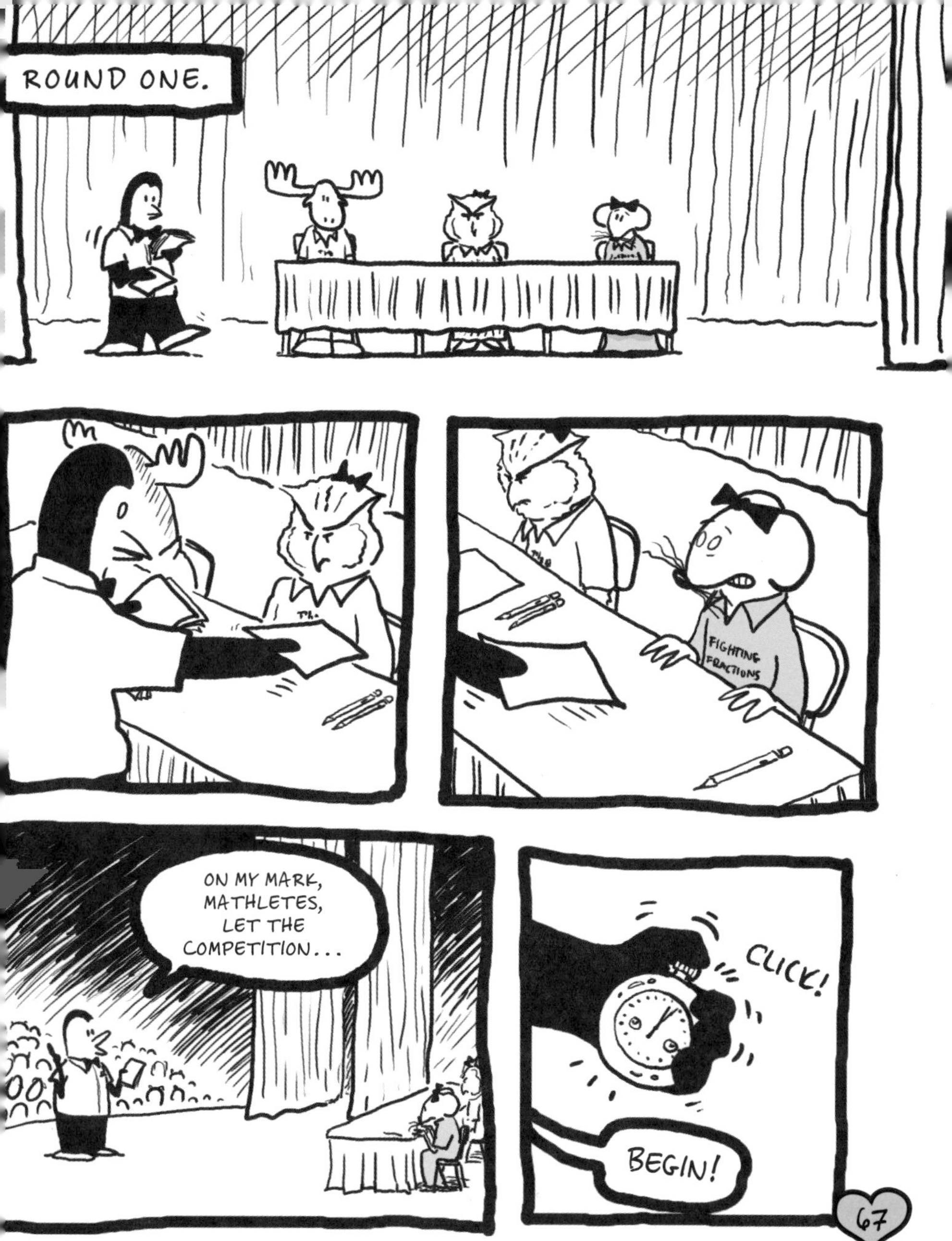
ROUND ONE.
FIGHTING FRACTIONS
ON MY MARK, MATHLETES, LET THE COMPETITION...
CLICK!
BEGIN!

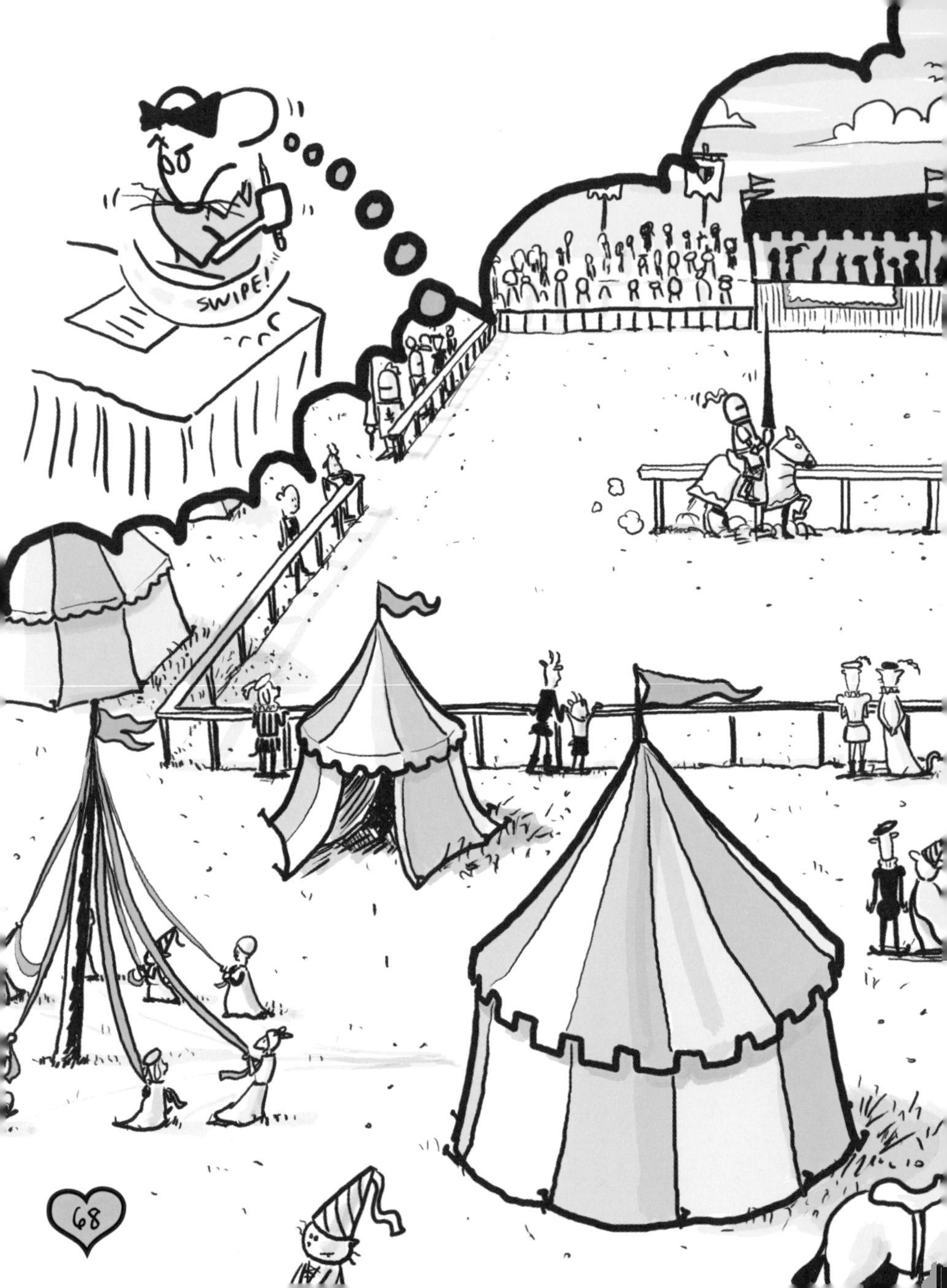
SWIPE!

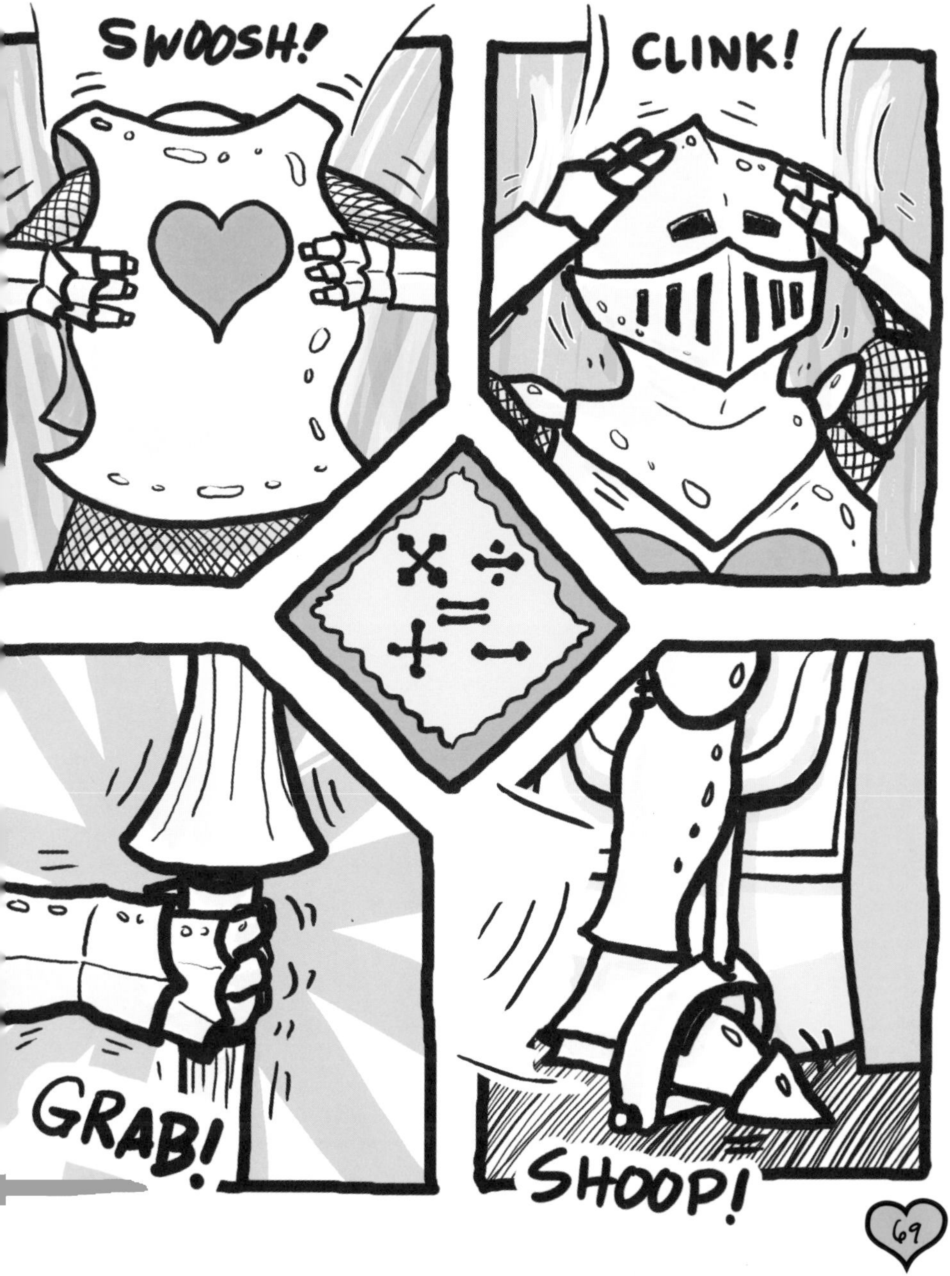
SWOOSH!
CLINK!
GRAB!
SHOOP!

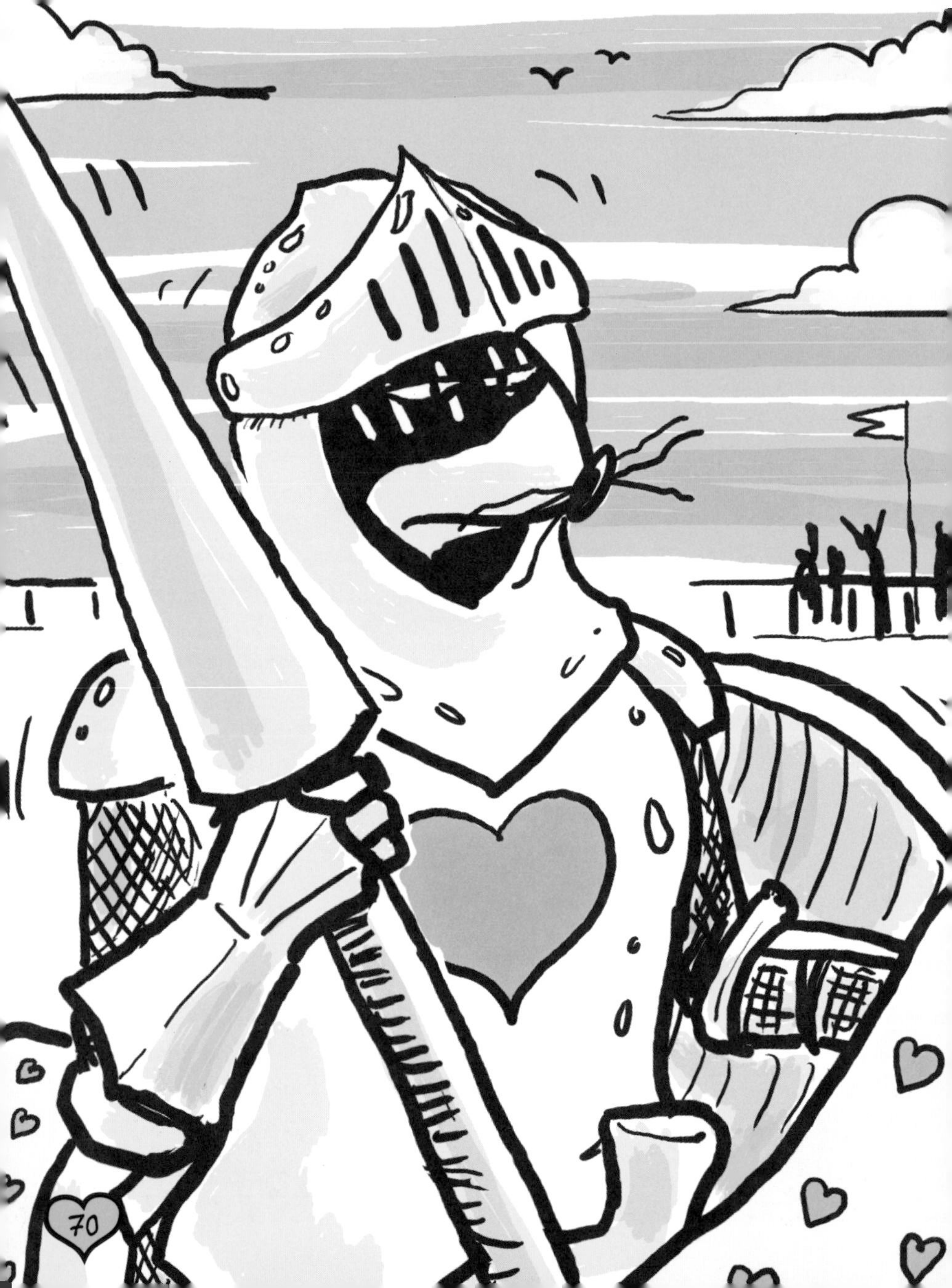

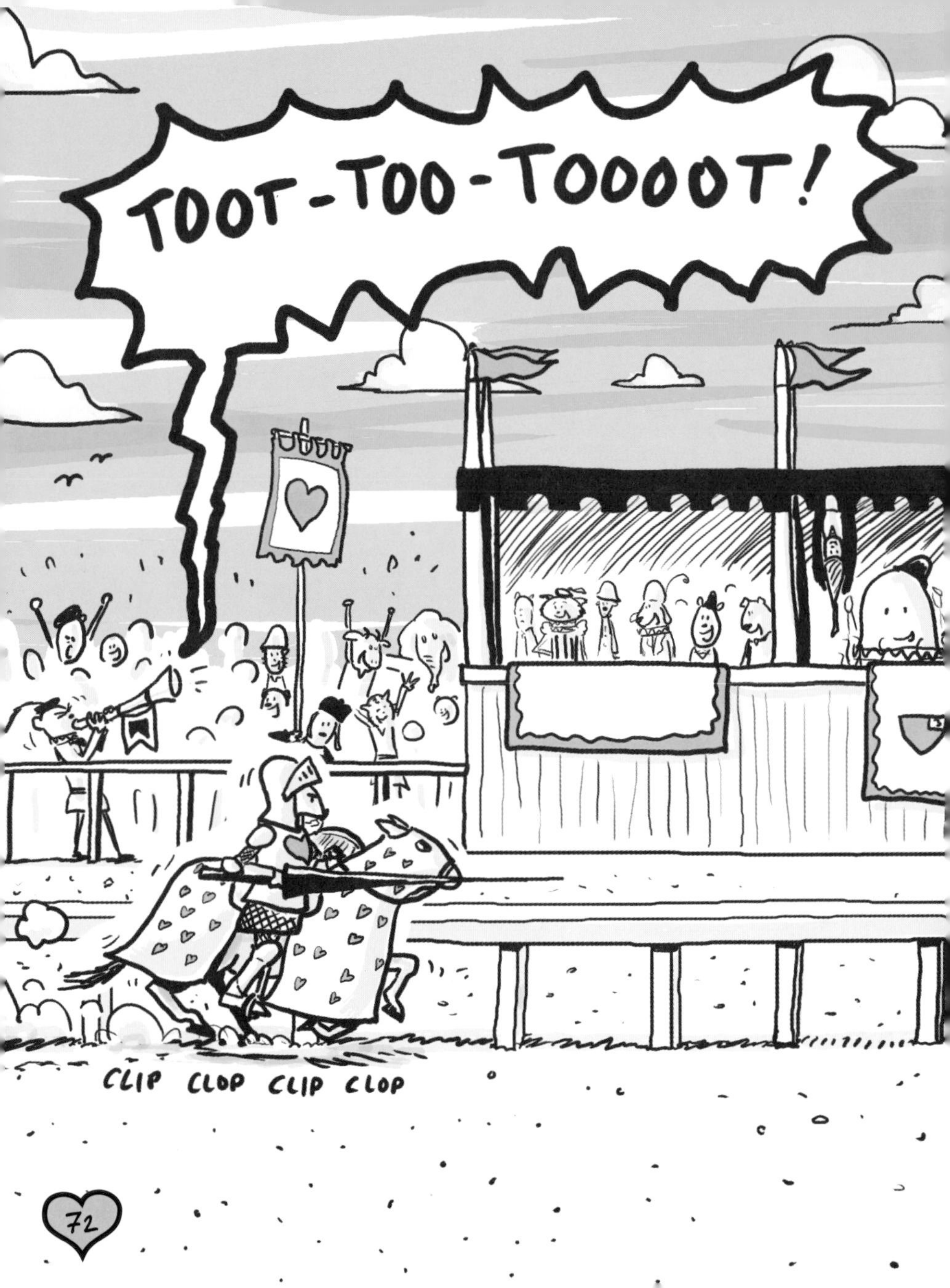
TOOT-TOO-TOOOOT!
CLIP CLOP CLIP CLOP

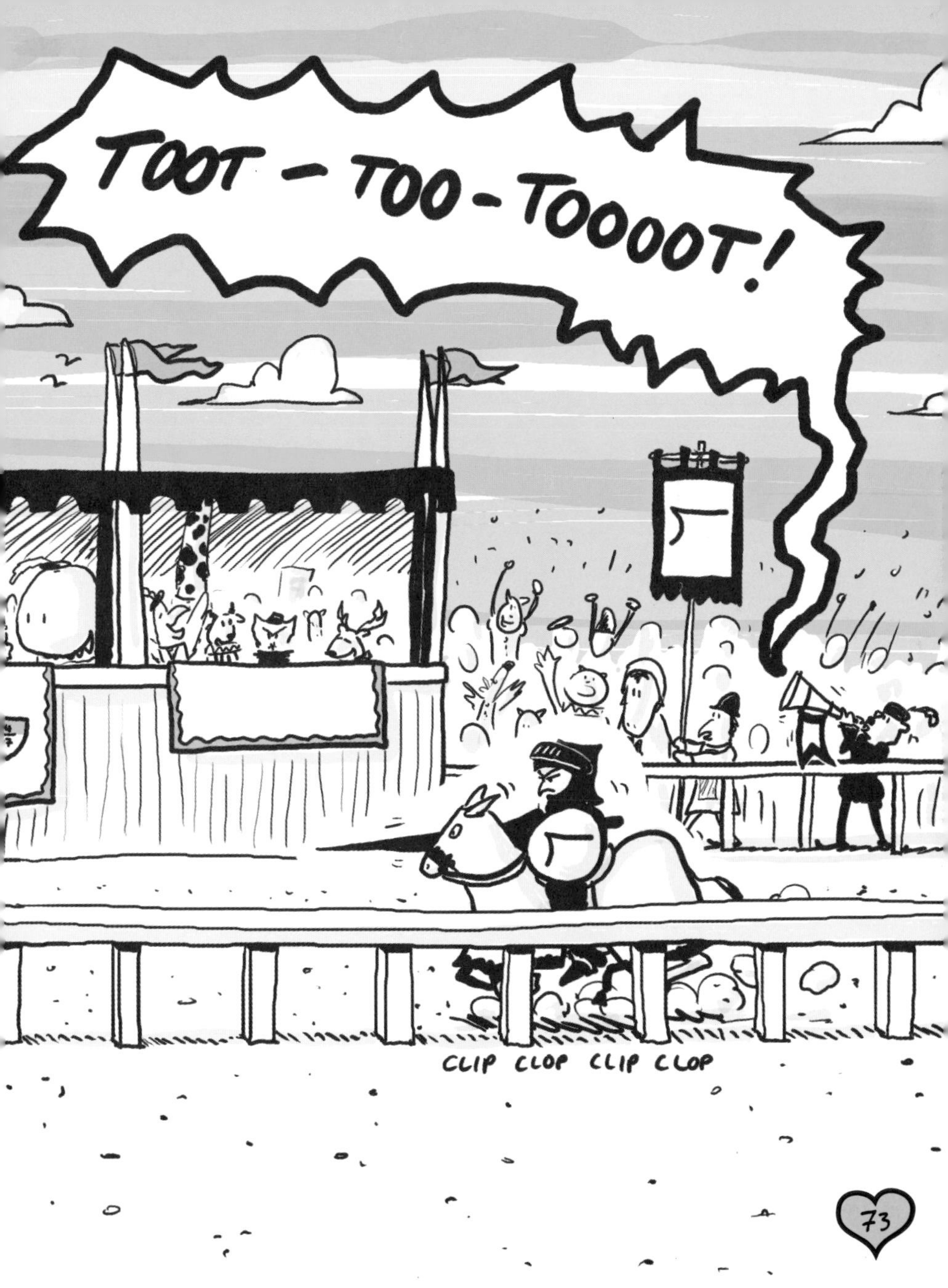
TOOT - TOO - TOOOOT!
CLIP CLOP CLIP CLOP

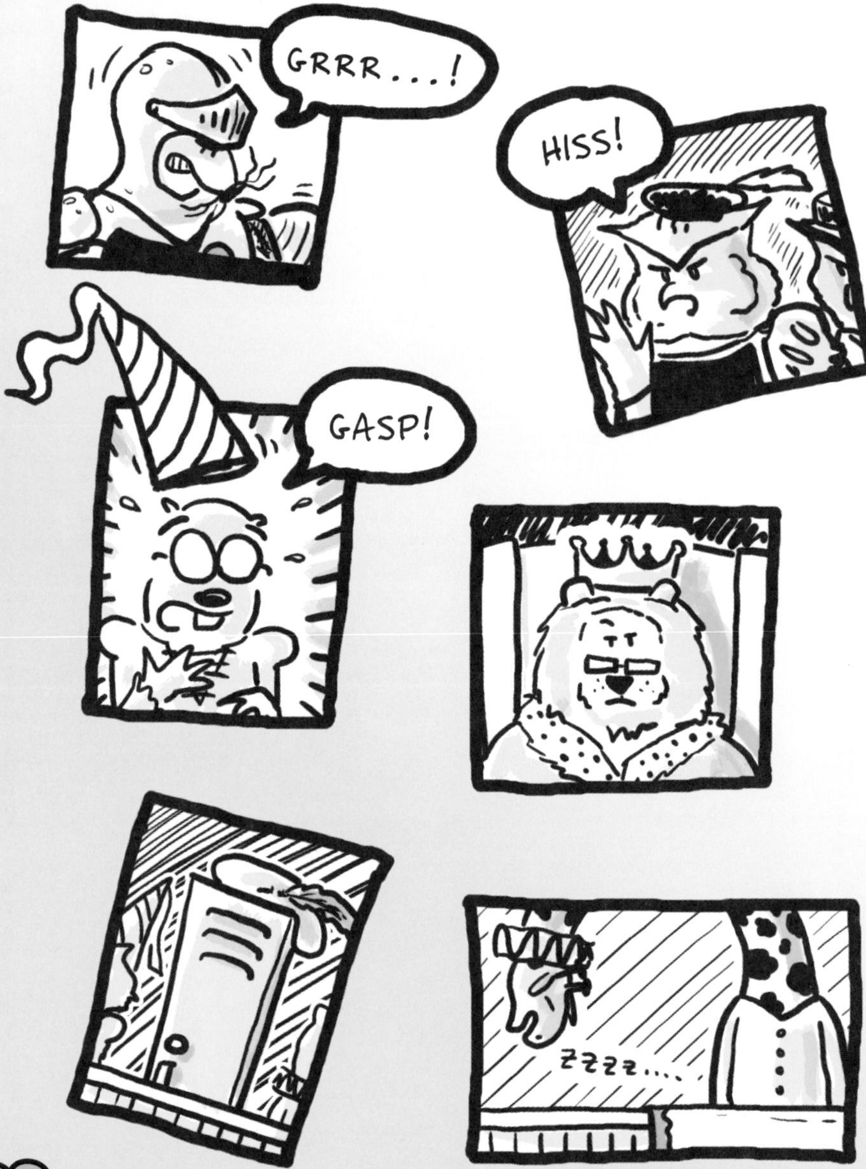
GRRR...!
HISS!
GASP!
ZZZZ....

HOOT HOOT! THAT WAS A CLASSIC! HOOT
HOOT! HOOT! WHAT DO YOU EXPECT FROM
FILTHY, DIRTY, DISEASE-CARRYING ROD
HOOT HOOT HOOT! ALL THEY'RE GOOD FO
SNACKS! HOOT! HOOT! HOOT! HA! WHAT'V
I'VE NEVEP   ᴘATHETI
HOOT HOᴏ   ᴇN GEᵀ
INTO THᴇ   ᴏT! Hᵀ
DO THEY   RY FOᵀ
KINDERGARTNERS? HOᴏ
GET A BODY BAG! HOOT
WAS THE QUICKEST LOSᵀ
THE WORLD! HOOT! HOOᵀ
A⟨76⟩ THIS TALK ABOUT

FORSOOTH, KNAVE—
THOU HAST FALLEN IN
THE MIRE.

YEA, VERILY.
UGH.

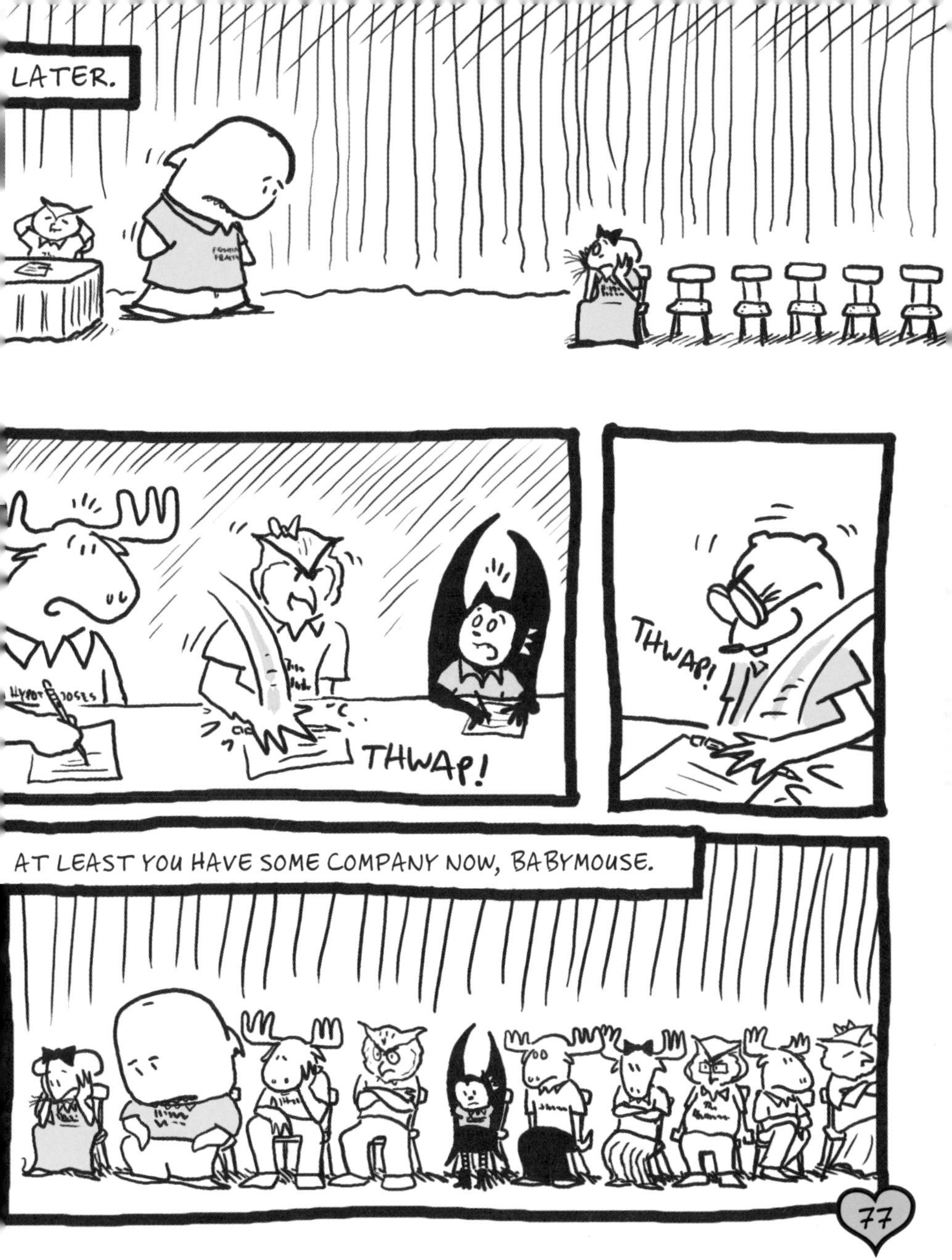

LATER.
THWAP!
THWAP!
AT LEAST YOU HAVE SOME COMPANY NOW, BABYMOUSE.

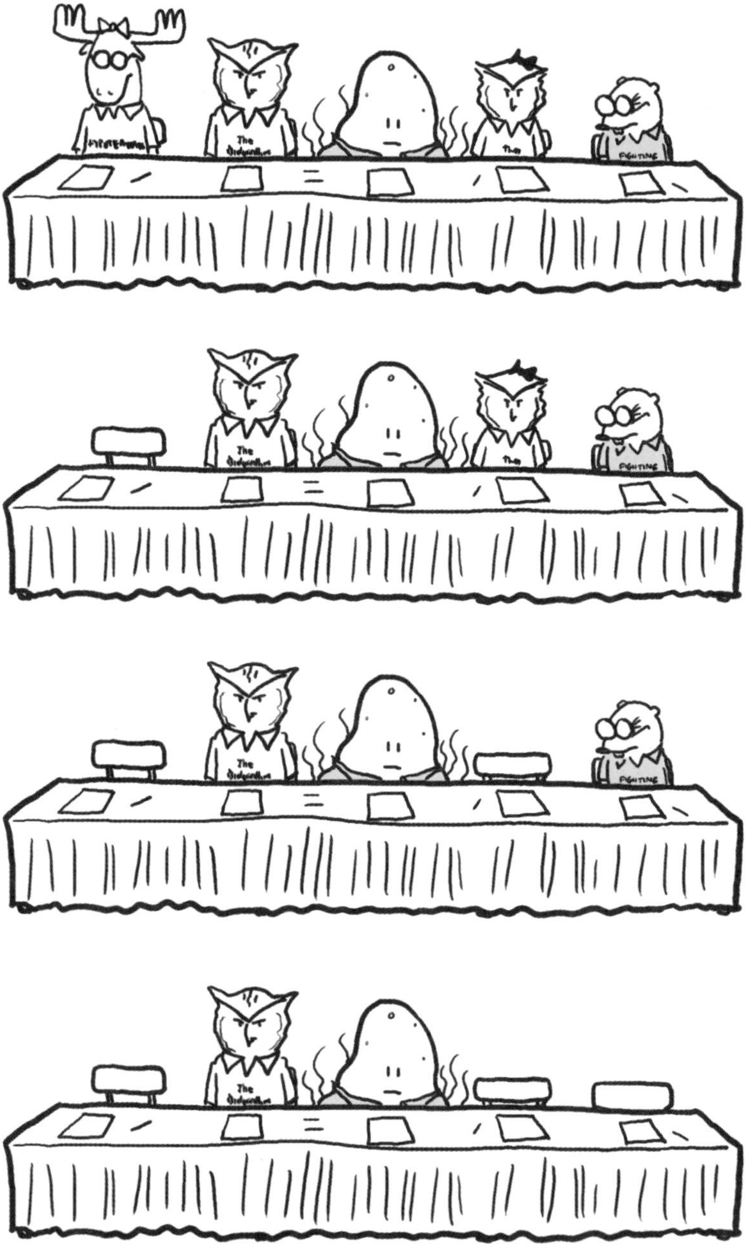

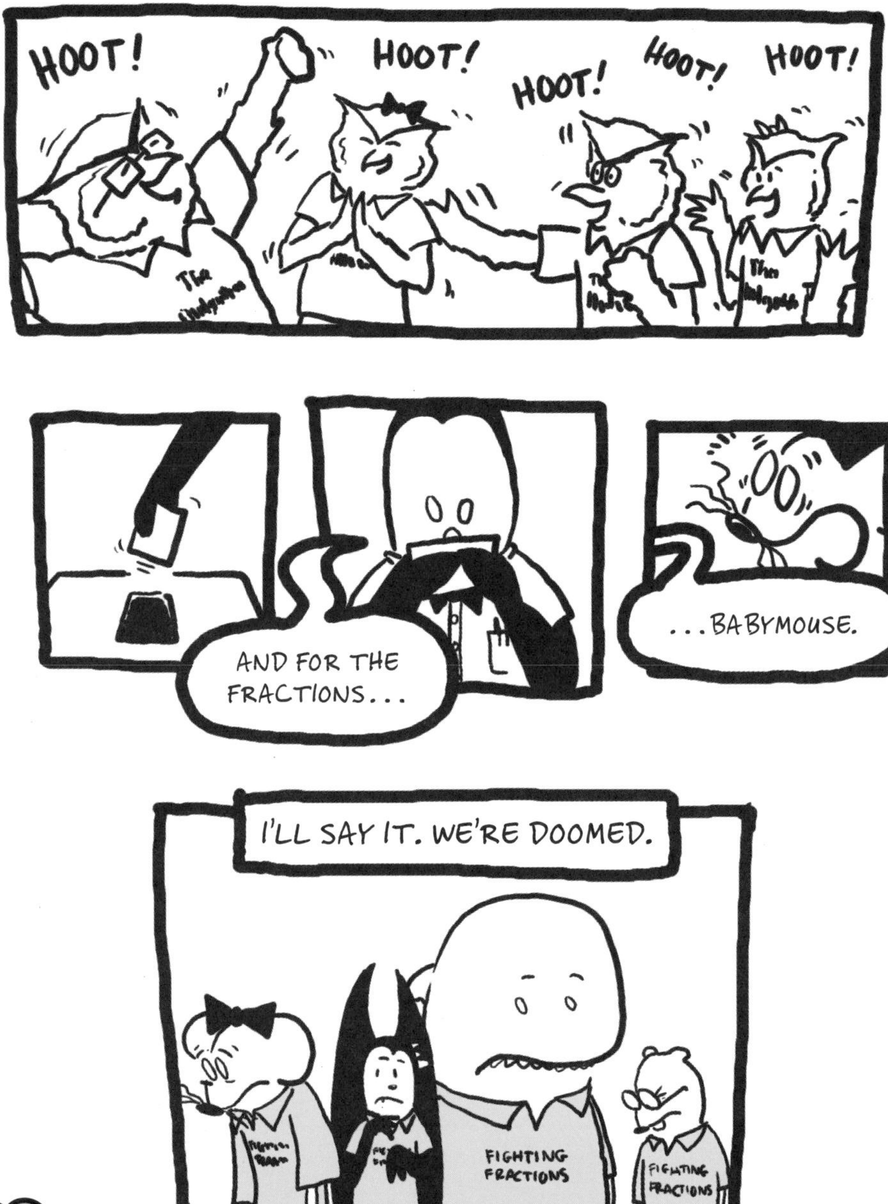
HOOT!
HOOT!
HOOT!
HOOT!
HOOT!
AND FOR THE FRACTIONS...
...BABYMOUSE.
I'LL SAY IT. WE'RE DOOMED.
FIGHTING FRACTIONS
FIGHTING FRACTIONS

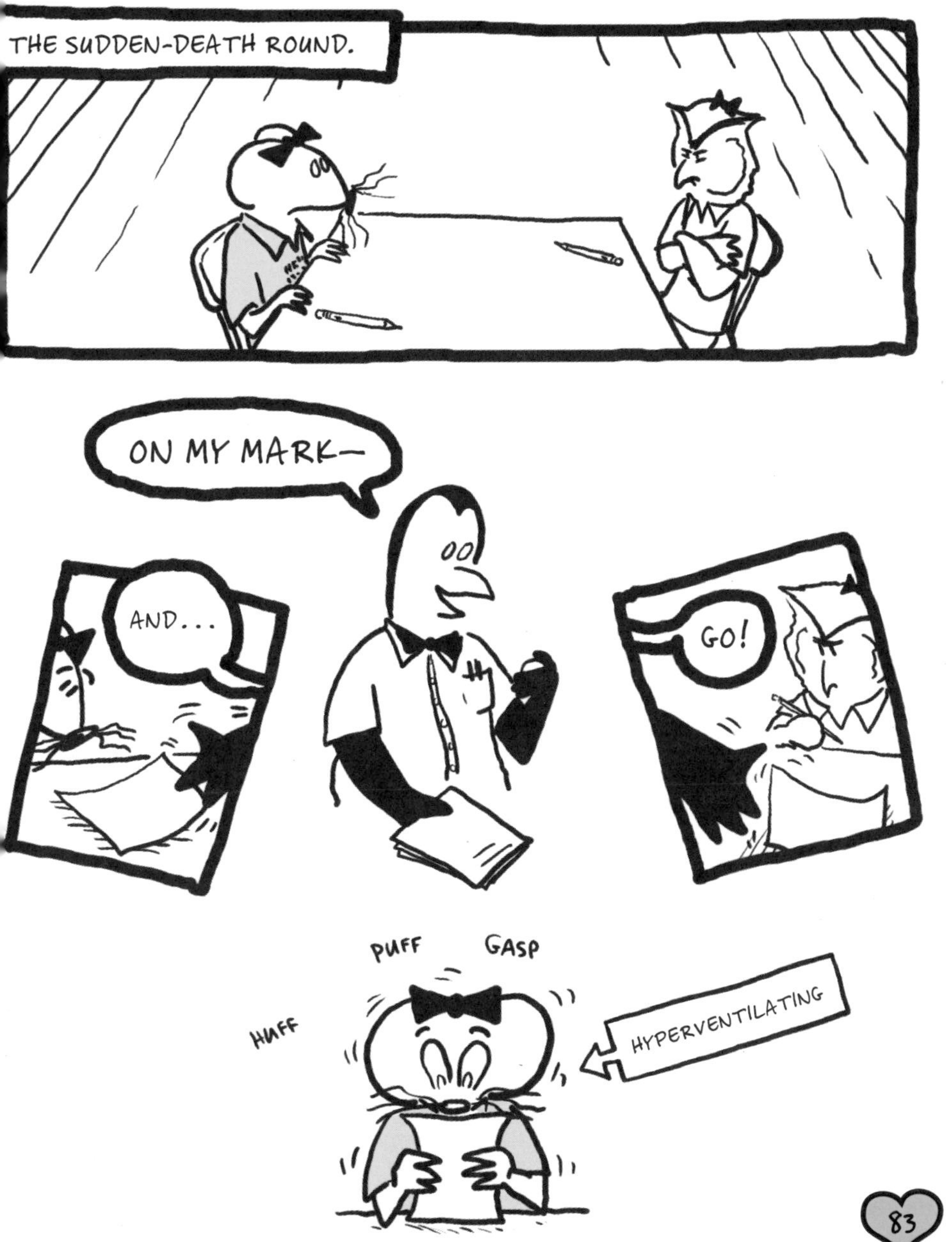
THE SUDDEN-DEATH ROUND.
ON MY MARK—
AND...
GO!
PUFF
GASP
HUFF
HYPERVENTILATING

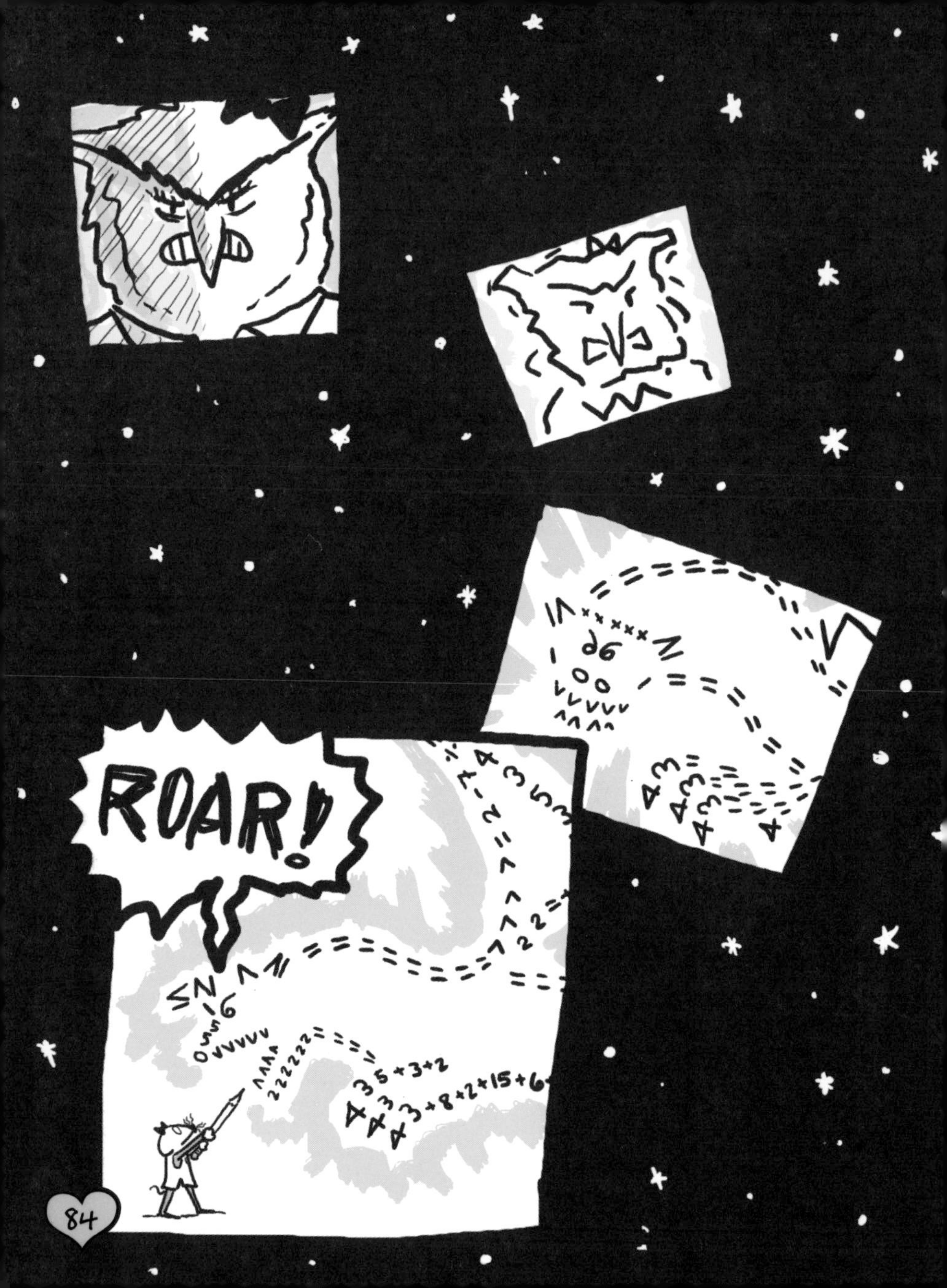
ROAR!

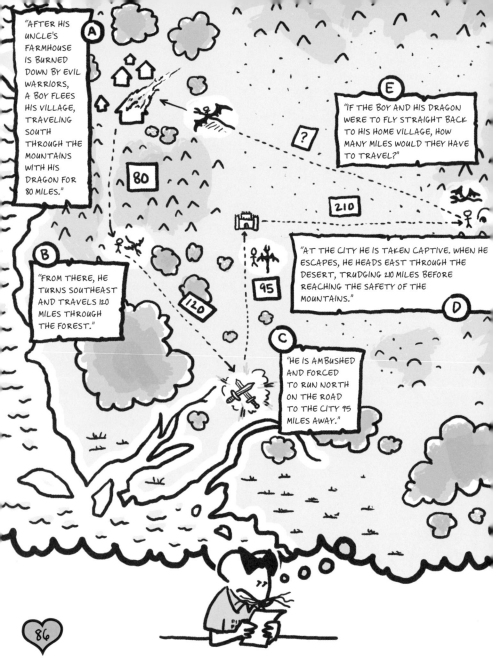

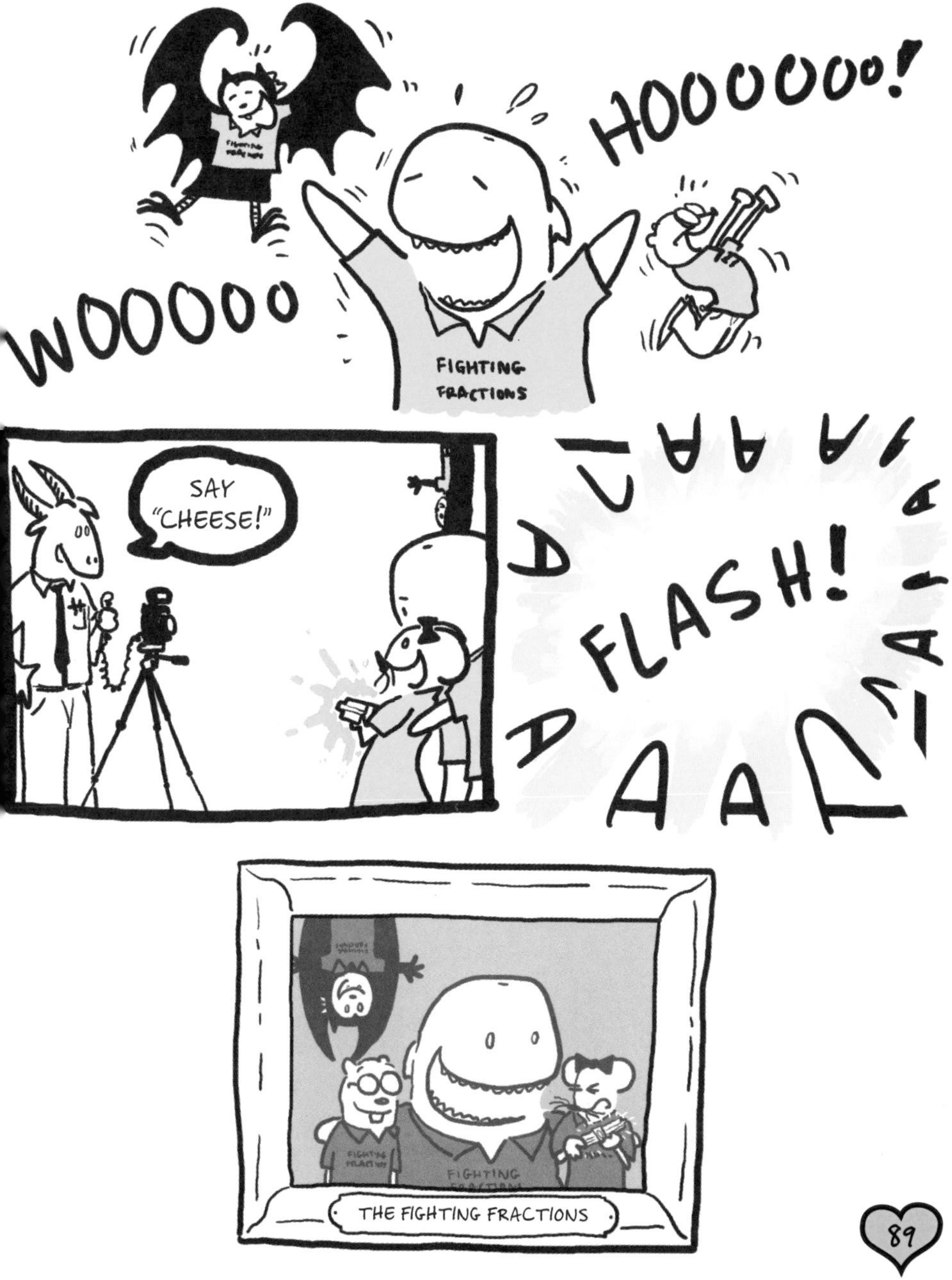

WOOOOO HOOOOOO!
FIGHTING FRACTIONS
SAY "CHEESE!"
FLASH!
FIGHTING FRACTIONS
THE FIGHTING FRACTIONS

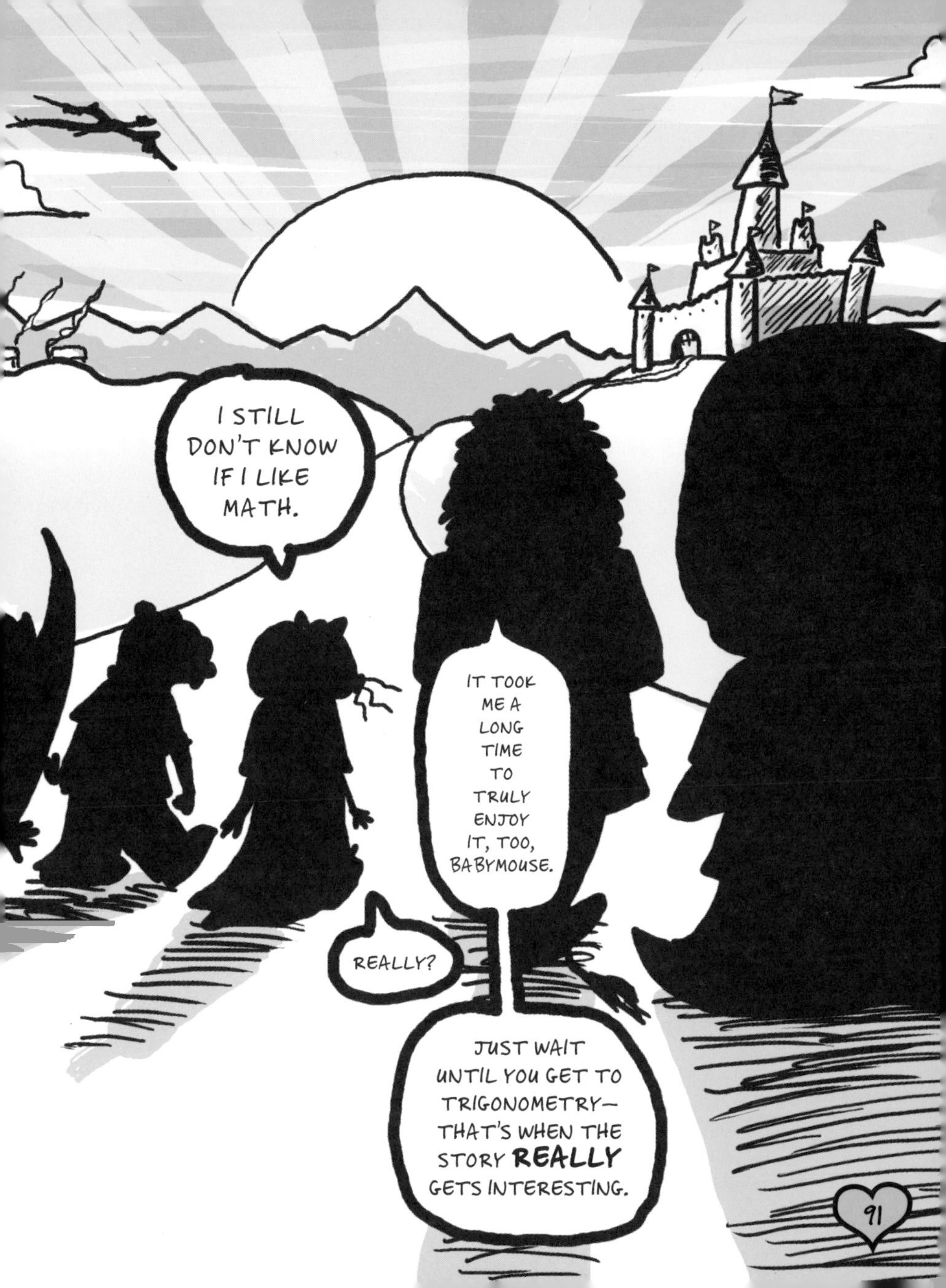
I STILL DON'T KNOW IF I LIKE MATH.
IT TOOK ME A LONG TIME TO TRULY ENJOY IT, TOO, BABYMOUSE.
REALLY?
JUST WAIT UNTIL YOU GET TO TRIGONOMETRY— THAT'S WHEN THE STORY **REALLY** GETS INTERESTING.

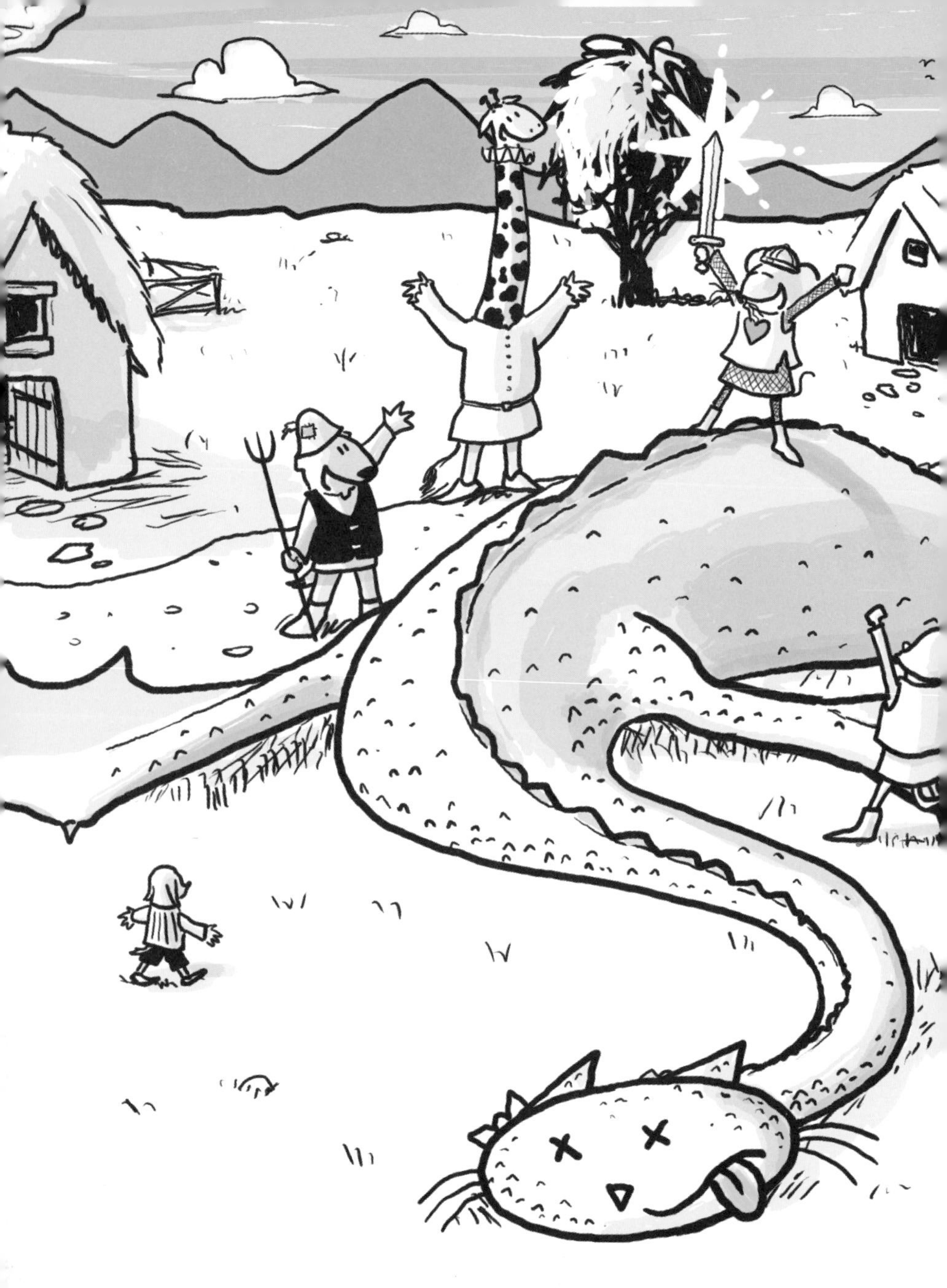

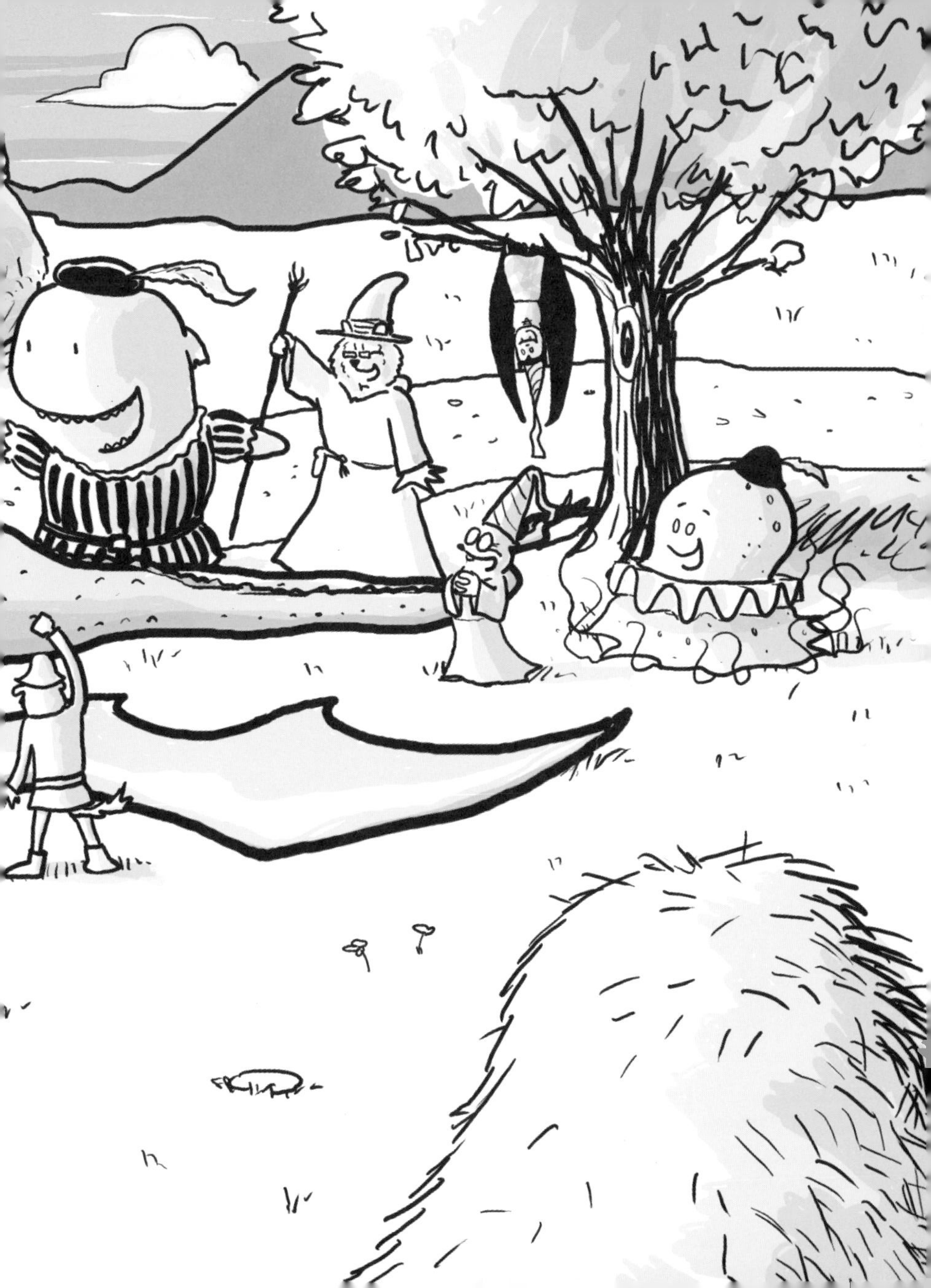